G STREET CHRONICLES PRESENTS

BLOCKED IN

by George Sherman Hudson

Typesetting: Shawna A. Grundy, TypesetMyBook
sag@shawnagrundy.com

LCCN: 2010915306
ISBN: 978-09826543-8-5

Join us on Facebook G Street Chronicles Fan Page

BLOCKED IN

DEDICATION

This book is dedicated to all my friends and family that continue to support me in my journey to make my mark in this publishing business.

ACKNOWLEDGMENT

I want to thank God for giving me the strength and wisdom to make my dreams come true despite my circumstances. I want to thank moms and pops for having my back through tough times. I also want to thank my special lady for keeping me motivated and focused in my mission. To all my kids Jazmine, Lil Sherman and Semaj, I love yall! To my patna Block who this book was named after, its your time bro do your thang. To my patna Cole Hart from Executive Urban Authors, bro as you and I know persistence and determination wins every time. To all my family and friends thanks for the support. To the G Street Chronicles family, its our time. To all the people who help bring these books to life: Publisher Nicola of NCM Publishing, Autumn, and my so talented graphic designer Vonda. I appreciate all yall hard work!

Chapter 1

"Come on now, sweetie. You can do what I say, or I can just take you back in the house and make your mama pay me what she owe me!" the old, frail crack head told Nikole through clenched teeth as they sat in his old beat-up station wagon in front of the rooming house.

Nikole was only fourteen years old and had been with over fifty men from all walks of life, thanks to her mother Gloria's drug addiction. Gloria had no problem offering them sex with Nikole in exchange for drugs. It had gotten to the point where Nikole was sleeping with more than three different strangers a day.

Gloria was a good mother up until she was intro-duced to cocaine by one of her White coworkers at the hospital where she worked as a registered nurse. She was one beautiful woman. Her olive skin, stripper body and big brown eyes had all the men in College Park nipping at her heels.

Nick was the only man she felt was worthy of her undivided attention. He was a ladies' man and one of Atlanta's most feared hustlers. Nick had introduced Gloria to a life of fame and fortune, a far cry different from her roots of poverty. Gloria was pregnant with their daughter Nikole when Nick shot and killed a man for trying to rob him. For defending himself, Nick was sentenced to life in prison, shattering Gloria's world.

Gloria was used to Nick taking care of her, and she never had to fend for herself before, but with him in jail and her being pregnant, she had to do something. She enrolled in medical school and became an RN. After a six-month stint as an intern in the local hospital, she was hired full-time, and she gave birth to Nikole shortly thereafter.

Gloria was a good mother that showered her baby

girl with only the best money could buy. When Nikole turned thirteen, though, she saw a huge change in her once loving, caring mother. The once gorgeous, well-kept Gloria turned into an underweight, foul-smelling stranger, demanding that her own daughter sleep with different men, threatening Nikole that if she didn't do it, the men she owed money to would kill her. Gloria's $10-a-day habit turned into a $100-a-day habit almost overnight, and having spent all of her savings and retirement funds, she started taking out loans and running up her credit cards to support her expensive addiction.

As if things could get any worse, a year later, jobless and penniless, Gloria's cocaine habit turned into a crack habit. After the bank foreclosed on their modest three-bedroom home, mother and daughter were forced to move into a rundown rooming house out in College Park, Georgia.

Nikole often thought of her father, though she never knew his whereabouts. Whenever she asked her mother about it, Gloria changed the subject. Nikole constantly prayed that one day, her father would come and save her and her mother from the vicious men who took advantage of Gloria's addictions and Nikole's young body. She often found herself sitting bored and lonely and terrified in their cramped, nasty room, watching as her mother sat at the rusty desk in the corner, getting high with different men day in and day out. The strangers were mostly men that would constantly stare at her with a sick lust in their eyes as they sucked on the glass pipe.

Nikole frequently thought back on the day it all started. She had just turned thirteen, and it was two days before Christmas. Nikole was lying across the bed she and Gloria shared, dressed in shorts and a t-shirt, watching cartoons. Her mother came through the door with another one of her strangers. The big 300-pound Black man was all sweaty and smelly. Paying them no mind, Nikole continued to watch TV until she heard her mother scream in the back of the room. The big man had her mother by the throat, choking her and demanding the money she owed him. Gloria fought to get free, and when she did, she quickly started to strip out of all her clothes. Nikole laid there, stunned, and watched as her mother stood in front of the sweaty big Black man, naked and frail, begging him to sleep with her in exchange for the money she owed him.

The big Black man then grabbed Gloria's naked, scrawny body and tossed her to the side, bringing his focus on Nikole, who was very developed for her age. He found her quite attractive sprawled across the bed in her shorts and a thin t-shirt.

Noticing the man's focus on her, Nikole quickly turned away and pretended to watch TV as she discreetly watched him through the corner of her eye.

Focusing back on Gloria, the man reached over, snatched her up, and whispered something in her ear. When Gloria nodded her head *yes*, the vile man reached into his pocket and pulled out a plastic bag that contained eight little white rocks. He plucked two of the small white pebbles out and handed them to Gloria as he began to undress. Before the big man was out of his pants, Gloria was in the corner inhaling the smoke that streamed out of the glass pipe that contained the rocks.

Nikole watched out of the corner of her eye as the overweight, sweaty man got completely naked and demanded the glass pipe from Gloria. After filling his lungs with the smoke, he cocked his head back, closed his eyes, and exhaled. The smoke faded into the air. After taking another hit, he gave the glass pipe back to Gloria and started across the room to where Nikole lay. Before the young girl could react, he was on top of her, trying to pull her shorts down. After becoming frustrated at her resistance, he roughly snatched her shorts to the side and shoved his fully erect manhood into Nikole, who screamed at the top of her lungs.

Nikole fought her heart out, to no avail, as her once-beloved mother just sat in the corner smoking her glass pipe while the big man raped her daughter over and over again, and from that day on, Nikole would see her mother Gloria in a completely different light.

Seeing Nikole as currency, a way to pay for her high, Gloria solicited her on a daily basis without so much as a shred of guilt or care; the smoke from the glass pipe was her one true love, even more valuable to her than the daughter her beloved and now incarcerated Nick had given her. As the months went on, Nikole was forced by her mother to sleep with man after man.

One evening, while a tearful Nikole sat on the front steps of the rooming house, a dark-skinned, bald-headed guy pulled up in a fancy SUV and asked the girl her name. She answered him and then got up to go back in the house, where her mother and yet another stranger were busy smoking crack.

The bald-headed gentleman's interest was piqued as he took in the curves Nikole's body yielded at such a young age. Before she got inside, the gentleman got out of the SUV, gently tugged on her elbow, and insisted she confide in him, and she did. She told him about the drugs, the different men, and her drugged-out mother. A few minutes later, she found herself in the passenger seat of the fancy SUV, headed to what this man promised would be a safer place for her. He introduced himself as 'Block,' and while he seemed like a savior to Nikole, what she didn't know was that he was one of the biggest pimps in the city of Atlanta.

Chapter 2

Block ran one of Atlanta's most profitable call-girl services, catering to the nation's rich and famous. He had come a long way from pimping school-age girls up and down the strip of Stewart Avenue in Atlanta to setting up escorts for dates with some of the wealthiest men—married and single—in the country. Block was stern in his ways, and he constantly threw his six-one, 220-pound frame around as intimidation. He quite literally ran his call-girl service with an iron fist.

The girls he employed were taught class and etiquette by Bella, who he referred to as his 'bottom broad.' Bella schooled all the new recruits on the proper ways to carry themselves amongst the rich and famous. Bella had been down with Block from day one. She was his first street walker, and after years of putting in work and paying her dues, Block retired her from the streets and made her his bottom broad. Block trusted Bella with his life. She was solid as a rock, and on top of that, she was a classy lady who was known to get gangster when it was called for.

Block made sure all of his women had only the best. The women he employed drove only the latest automobiles, lived in palatial homes, and were adorned only in top-of-the-line clothes. Every female that worked for Block was considered top notch. He only dealt with girls he considered to be 'eye candy.'

Block was in his late forties, but he looked years younger. He was a true ladies' man. Anyone who ran across him would more than likely peg him as a stockbroker or some kind of business professional. He always dressed casually and spoke with intelligence. He frequented many social gatherings to seek out potential clientele.

Years earlier, when Block was in the midst of

establishing his service, he caught some girls trying to reach out to clients after hours, which was a breach of trust, and it called for termination. He got rid of numerous girls simply because of disloyalty. One evening, on the way to pick his clothes up from the dry cleaner, he peeped a young girl in distress and knew from the low-income area where he found her that she would not refuse a helping hand and a better lifestyle. When he approached her and consoled her to gain her confidence, she accepted his offer of a better life. That girl was Nikole.

Chapter 3

Five Years Later

"This is so generous of you," Nikole told Reverend Kyle, head of one of Atlanta's most prestigious churches and husband of thirty years, as she folded the seven one-hundred-dollar bills he tipped her with and stuck them in her purse.

The reverend was one of Block's highest-paying clients and spent generously for every date. Like all of Block's clients, Reverend Kyle had a special account with an active credit card on file that was charged before every date. Once, when Nikole was out of town with a high-paying politician, the good reverend contacted Block for her services. Block told him she was unavailable and suggested a replacement, but the reverend declined, only wanting Nikole. Block really hated to lose out on the $2,500 he would have charged to the reverend's account, just for one night.

As time went on, Block noticed more than half of his high-paying clients only requested Nikole for dates. Nikole herself was bringing in more than all the other girls combined. Block really couldn't blame them because Nikole had grown to be every man's dream. Her long legs and apple-shaped backside were far from all she had to offer. Standing five-seven with some of the smoothest olive-hued skin and big light brown eyes, all with an intellect to match, she was a total package. Block referred to her as 'the Black Kim Kardashian.' He never brought to her attention her worth, which was easily seven figures a year. She alone had made him a millionaire. Nikole was Block's bread and butter, his meal ticket.

"I hope to see you next week," Nikole told Reverend Kyle as they exited the plush five-star hotel and headed to their cars.

As Nikole entered her brand new sky blue Aston Martin Coupe, she checked her lipstick in the mirror and put in her Sade CD. She waved and blew the reverend a kiss as he drove by, exiting the parking lot in his big black Mercedes Benz.

On the outside, it seemed Nikole was happy with the life she lived, but on the inside, twenty-year-old Nikole was lonely and utterly unhappy. She always thought money would bring her happiness, but after becoming very wealthy, she saw it wasn't what she thought it would be.

Turning out of the parking lot, she headed to Block's house, where he was having a get-together for all of his girls. Nikole loved Block like a father. He had taken her in at fourteen years of age when she had nothing, not even an education. He had Bella home school her while he schooled her on the ins and outs of the street. He sent her out on her first date when she was just sixteen years old, with one of his first wealthy clients. The young, nerdy architect requested her for the following three weekends. Nikole had handled herself like a real vet in the game, which made Block proud. Nikole trusted him completely; he had saved her from a life of misery and given her her every dream. At seventeen years old, she had a three-bedroom home out in the affluent area of Atlanta, a brand new convertible BMW, and a bank account just shy of $100,000. Now, at twenty years old, she had the car of her dreams, a mini-mansion out in Buckhead, and seven figures invested in stocks and bonds. She thanked Block every morning when she woke up and every night before she went to sleep. The man was her God.

Gloria was a merely distant memory in Nikole's mind. She sometimes wondered what had become of her mother. Every time she passed the old rooming house, she tried to look and see if there were signs of Gloria still there. Deep down, she really loved her mother, but on the surface, the hatred was strong. As she grew older, though, she became more aware of the effects of drugs on a weak individual, which she considered her mother to be.

Chapter 4

Every time Nikole visited East Wood Estates, she was always amazed by the size of the multimillion-dollar homes divided by well-manicured acres of land. After turning a few blocks, she pulled up in front of Block's mansion that sat a few yards back from the iron security gates that were custom-inscribed with a big gold 'B' in the center. She buzzed the intercom, and the big gates slowly opened.

Parking her Aston in the eight-car garage, Nikole checked her appearance to make sure there were no flaws. When she reached the top of the steps, she was greeted at the door by Bella, who looked way younger than her forty-two years.

Bella stood five-two and was bow legged and petite with long, wavy golden hair and skin dark as night. She was the true definition of a 'boss bitch.' She took no shit off anyone, Block included. Bella had been like a mother to Nikole and taught her how to be a strong, classy woman. "Hey, baby! Glad you could make it!" Bella told Nikole as she opened the door and greeted her with a hug.

"It's good to see you, girl. You still looking good," Nikole replied, embracing her a second time.

"Come on in," said Bella, stepping aside to let Nikole by.

The mansion was breathtaking. It was tastefully decorated by one of Atlanta's most sought-after interior designers. Block had a thing for black and gold, which was splayed all throughout the house. The marble floors were even accented with black and gold specks.

The walls were covered with some of the most expensive paintings and artifacts that dated back centuries. Security cameras were positioned in every corner and were constantly monitored by the on-site security guard. The furnishings alone were worth more than a million dollars.

The guests were downstairs in the entertainment room that housed an over sized black leather couch that stretched from wall to wall. The seventy-two-inch Sony flat-screen TV took up the whole far wall, while the in-wall shark tank took up the other. In between the two were Block's center of attraction—his custom black and gold pool table with a big gold 'B' in the center. Across from his center of attraction was his custom gold and black chess set with two gold and black leather chairs flanking both sides.

The girls were playing pool and watching TV when Nikole entered the room.

"Hey, Nikole!" screamed a thick, green-eyed, half-breed sista from across the room.

"Hey, China!" Nikole replied as they embraced for a sisterly hug. "How have you been doing?" Nikole inquired, happy to see China after a year.

"Working, girl—in and out of the country. Block got me all over Canada on dates," she sighed. "What about you? How you doing?"

"Same as you, but I ain't got that global clientele like you," Nikole joked.

"Girl, please don't even go there."

"Just messing with you. Where Block at?" asked Nikole, looking around the room for him.

"I ain't seen him. I just got here too. Cream, you seen Block?" China yelled across the room to a chocolate, slim, curvy sista that resembled Tyra Banks.

"Naw, he ain't been down here since I been here," she replied as she flipped the channel on the flat-screen TV.

There were a total of twelve girls present, and the other eight were out on dates. Block made it his business to bring all of his girls together as a family once every six months. At each gathering, a new girl was added to the family. He would introduce her to every girl one by one, his way of letting her see that everyone was happy, well off, and—most importantly—loyal to him.

Nikole was familiar with most of the faces around the room; a few she knew very well. She had had a confrontation with this one Jamaican sista that was jealous of her position in the family. She felt as if Block catered to Nikole and treated her better than everyone else. She constantly complained about how Nikole always ended up on dates with the wealthier clients. Nikole and the girl were inches away from getting physical at the last get-together until Bella stepped in between them. Later, when Block heard about it, he pulled Jamaica to the side, and after that, Nikole never heard anything else from her. Now, every time she saw Jamaica, she was faced with a mean look and some rolling eyes.

As the evening went on, Nikole and China sipped on some Nuvo and told each other stories about past dates.

Just as Nikole was about to tell her the story about her date with a rich cripple, Block entered the room. "Ladies! Ladies! Ladies!" he chanted as he walked through the door, looking around the room at all the beautiful women—all *his* beautiful women.

Block was adorned in slacks and a silk button-up. He walked around the room, hugging all of his investments. Block had carefully recruited every single girl in the room and changed all of their lives for the better. He had made each and every one of them wealthy. "How all of my family doing?" he called out as he circled the room.

"Good... Fine!" all the girls yelled.

After making his rounds and introducing his new family member, he called Nikole out to the indoor pool house.

"What's wrong, Block? Everything okay?" Nikole asked curiously.

"No problems at all. I just wanted to let you know I appreciate all your hard work and loyalty."

"Oh. Thanks, Block, but I should be thanking you. You saved my life," Nikole replied, her eyes beginning to tear up.

"I want to do something special for you. I'm going to give you some days off, and I'm sending you to Las Vegas for the weekend, my treat."

Nikole was surprised because Block was known for being generous, but not for giving any of his girls time off. "Oh, Block! Thanks!" she replied excitedly, hugging him and thinking about all the fun she was going to have in the casinos.

"You deserve it, baby girl," Block told her as he thought about the big convention coming up, knowing all his most wealthy clients who loved

Nikole were going to be in attendance. Block wanted her to get as much rest as possible in Vegas, because when she returned, she would be working nonstop during the convention.

Chapter 5

Taking her seat in the first-class section of the American Airlines jumbo jet, Nikole pulled out her book, *Drama*, by one of her favorite authors and got comfortable. As she reached the third chapter, her eyes grew heavy. She fought long and hard, but sleep overcame her, and she dozed off with book in hand. When she came to, the 'Fasten Your Seatbelt' signs were blinking; they were landing in Vegas.

After getting off the plane, Nikole headed straight for the conveyor belt to retrieve her signature Gucci luggage. While waiting on her bags, she looked around for some of the famous people that frequented

Vegas. This was not Nikole's first trip to Vegas, but it was her first trip there without the burden of trying to entertain and satisfy someone other than herself. Grabbing her Gucci bags, she headed to the rental car counter.

Nikole wasn't surprised when the convertible Jaguar in Block's signature black rounded the corner. Exchanging pleasantries with the driver, she waited as he exited the driver seat and rechecked his checklist to make sure everything was in tact. After signing his checklist, Nikole positioned herself behind the wheel and headed to the MGM Grand, where her reserved luxury suite awaited her arrival.

A few minutes later, she was passing her keys off to the parking attendant at the MGM Grand and entering the luxurious five-star hotel. Still on the lookout for movie stars and celebrities, Nikole noticed how the wealthy mingled amongst each other, exchanging business cards and recommending the best gainers on the stock market.

Nikole stood in line behind an Arabian gentleman with a sista black as night on his arm. Being in the game so long, she knew the woman was his hired date, a sex toy for him to play with for the weekend. Seeing it from this angle made Nikole cringe at the thought of being someone's sex toy.

Finally, she reached the counter and recited her information to the blonde-haired, blue-eyed, well-tanned White woman who, in turn, handed her the keys to her suite, along with a toothy smile.

Entering the elevator and riding up to the twenty-fifth floor, Nikole couldn't wait to take full advantage of this all-expense-paid vacation. Exiting the elevator and locating her suite, Nikole wasted no time inserting her key into the door and entering her room for the weekend.

The suite was breathtaking. It had a balcony that jutted out over the Vegas strip that connected all the night clubs and casinos that people from all over the world flocked to. The suite had in-room spa amenities, a wet bar, and HD flat-screen TVs on the wall in front of the bed and in the dining area. After checking out the suite and its luxuries, Nikole pulled out her Blackberry and called Block.

"Speak," Block ordered as he answered the phone on the third ring.

"Hey, Block. I'm here and loving the accommodations you reserved for me. Thanks so much," Nikole said sincerely as she laid back on the king-sized bed with the phone to her ear.

"Anything for you, baby girl. Like I told you before, you have been outstanding and really deserved a vacation. Just don't go overboard in them casinos."

"Never! I'm not a gambler. I bet only on the sure thing," Nikole joked.

"Baby girl, go have a good time, and if you need me, just call."

"Thanks. Talk to you later."

After hanging up with Block, Nikole unpacked her bags and headed for the shower. She freshened up and put on a pair of olive skin-tight jeans, a form-fitting black top, and her black and olive Cavalli heels. She checked her hair and makeup in the bathroom mirror and then decided on a destination—the twenty-four-hour Studio Café. She had fallen in love with their seasoned chicken fingers and fries the last time she was in Vegas, on a date with a rich Jamaican client.

Taking a seat at the bar, she ordered chicken

fingers and a Nuvo with pineapple, her favorite. By the time she decided it was time to go, she had finished off two more glasses of Nuvo. Feeling good and slightly tipsy, she exited the café and headed to her room.

As she entered the lobby, she ran into a crowd of women surrounding a tall, light-skinned, bald-headed brother. Curious, she moved into the crowd and saw that the women were trying to get him to sign their books. As she looked closer, she realized the book was titled *Love Jones*, and this brother's face was on the back next to the 'About the Author' blurb. Satisfying her curiosity, she backed up out of the crowd and headed for the elevators.

She pushed the button and waited for the elevator, and she noticed the gentleman was headed in her direction, the crowd of fans still in tow. Stopping in his tracks, he turned and politely told all of his followers that he was having a book signing the next day at Barnes and Noble, and he would gladly answer all of their questions and sign all of their books then.

Nikole stepped into the elevator just as he finished

his speech. Just as the door was about to close, he stepped in and pressed '25,' the same button Nikole had pressed. They stood in awkward silence as the elevator headed up.

"Hi," he spoke, breaking the silence somewhere near the sixth floor.

"Hey," Nikole replied as she inhaled the sweet-smelling scent that was coming off the brother.

There was another brief silence as the elevator continued its upward journey.

Chapter 6

"Having fun yet?" the gentleman asked, trying to break the awkward silence once again, this time around the twelfth floor.

"It's all just starting. I just arrived a couple of hours ago," Nikole said, still feeling woozy off of the Nuvo and pineapple.

"So rude of me! My name is Curtis Conway," he said, extending his hand to Nikole.

"Nikole Jones." She smiled and shook his hand.

"May I ask where you are from, Ms. Jones?"

"That's *Miss* Jones, and I'm from College Park, Georgia," Nikole responded, checking out his broad shoulders and big hands.

"College Park!" Curtis called out.

"Yeah, Old National Highway, Flat Shoals Road... around that area," Nikole stated, trying to block out all the bad memories of her childhood there.

"I'm from College Park too! I grew up out on Godby Road in Limetree, right up from the Stop and Shop!" Curtis barked excitedly.

"What? I used to have a friend that stayed on Godby Road! We used to run out there in Bradford Square and in the plaza. Her name is Catressa—"

"Catressa Miller!" Curtis finished.

"You know Catressa?" Nikole asked excitedly.

"Hell yeah! Who don't know Catressa and her big mouth. She used to hang out with my sister all the time. I know her whole family—her dad Ed, who was country as hell, her big-mouth sister Tasha, whose husband drove trucks, her sister Christie, who moved to Valdosta, and their mother, Peggy, who had a wig for every day of the week. I know the Millers real well."

"Wow! What a small world!" Nikole declared as the elevator stopped on their floor.

"Are you here with someone?" Curtis asked as they exited the elevator.

"Nope—just me, myself, and I," Nikole told him softly as they walked down the narrow corridor to their suite. "What about you? You here by yourself?" Nikole asked while fishing her room key out of the pocket of her skin-tight jeans.

"No. I'm actually here with a friend. She's probably down in the casinos losing all her money as we speak," he responded as he watched Nikole's curves sway from side to side as she walked beside him.

"Oh, yeah, those casinos will get you caught up and suck you right in," Nikole said softly, disappointed in his reply.

"Well, it was nice meeting you, Nikole… home girl," Curtis said while looking into her big light brown eyes as he stopped in front of his suite and pulled his key out of his pants pocket.

"Same here," Nikole said as she continued to her suite at the end of the hallway.

When she reached her suite and stuck the key in to unlock the door, she couldn't help looking back in Curtis's direction; he was gone. She entered the suite and made her way to the bathroom and filled the oval-shaped tub with warm water. She stripped out of her clothes, got into the soapy water, laid her head back, and thought about Curtis. Everything about him had her turned on: the way he looked at her, his demeanor, his scent, the way he walked.

After soaking in the tub for close to an hour, Nikole got out, slipped on her boy shorts and tank top, and climbed into the king-sized bed that suddenly seemed too big for just one person. Lying there, lost in thought, she reached over and dialed Curtis's suite.

"Hello?" he answered.

Without saying a word, Nikole hung up and drifted off to sleep, not before blaming her attraction on the Nuvo and pineapple.

Chapter 7

After getting rid of her terrible hangover, Nikole dragged herself out of bed and made reservations at Christopher Salon for a full manicure and pedicure. After a long shower, she slipped on her bright red body-fitting sun dress and open-toed sandals. Exiting the suite and walking by Curtis's door, she thought about the previous night and her crazy attraction to this man she barely knew. She wrote it off again as a little too much Nuvo as she waited for the elevator to come to her floor.

A few minutes later, the light on the top of the elevator lit up, and the doors opened. Curtis made her heart skip a beat as he stood there in his all-white linen. "Hi, Nikole! We meet again," he said as his eyes fixated on Nikole's bulging hips and thick thighs that the tight sundress revealed.

"Yes we do," Nikole replied shyly.

"You in a hurry?" he asked as he held the elevator doors open.

"Yes and no. What's up?" Nikole asked curiously.

"Well, I'm working on this book and really need a female's point of view," he stated, stepping out of the elevator in front of her.

"Your friend couldn't give you the female point of view you're looking for?" Nikole said, trying hard not to sound jealous.

"She left this morning. She usually accompanies me on all of my book signings, making sure everything is situated with each venue. She's been with me since I started my company, Azure Books."

"Never mix business with pleasure," Nikole chimed in.

"Oh, it's nothing like that. We're more like family. She calls herself my 'traveling assistant.' She runs the company when I'm not available," Curtis explained as the elevator doors closed behind them.

"That's nice to hear. Well, I really was—"

"You're going to make me beg, I see," Curtis cut in as he started to kneel in front of her.

"No, no… get up! I can't be too long because I have an appointment for a manicure and pedicure shortly," Nikole told him as she looked up into his eyes when he stood, towering over her.

"I promise I won't keep you long," he assured her as he led the way to his suite.

Reaching his suite, he opened the door and stepped aside so Nikole could enter. He admire her goods as she walked past him into the suite over to the kitchen counter. His suite had the same floor plan as Nikole's, only his had books strewn all over the room, and an expensive laptop that was illuminated on the table in the TV room.

Nikole walked over to the TV room, where over 100 books were staked on the long oak table. "You wrote all of these?" Nikole asked, picking up three of the romance novels that had Curtis's picture plastered on the back covers.

"Yeah. I see you're not too familiar with my writings. You don't read much, do you?" Curtis asked, surprised that Nikole really didn't know his status—but also pleasantly surprised by that.

"No, not really. I'm way too busy," Nikole said as she looked over all the different books he had authored.

"That one right there was one of my bestsellers. The movie *Secret Attraction* was based on that book."

"No way! You got to be kidding! That is one of my favorite movies," Nikole declared excitedly.

"Yeah, seriously," Curtis added as he took a seat in front of his laptop.

"They always say the book is better than the movie. I got to read this," Nikole insisted.

"That is a true saying. Come check this out and tell me what you think," he said as he pulled a chair up next to him at the laptop.

Nikole read the words on the screen:

Sarah asked him, "How do you know when it's true love?" and he explained to her that true love is a love that is unbreakable, a love that lasts a lifetime, a love that never fades or has doubts, a love that you would give your life for, a love that is God sent...

Curtis watched Nikole's eyes as she read the

passage in his upcoming novel. The more she read, the more her heart pitter-pattered. As she reached the last sentence, she noticed Curtis watching her intently. "It's good. I like it," she said, slightly blushing.

"You take it all as truth, or do you think I need to change some of it?"

"No… it's… it's all… true," Nikole stammered.

"Have you ever encountered love like that?" Curtis asked as he locked his eyes on hers.

"Uh… no… I don't think I have," Nikole answered, somewhat embarrassed and looking away. "Well, it's about time I get going," she whispered as she slid her chair back away from the computer and his beautiful prose.

"Would you turn it away if it ever did come your way?"

"No. Why would anybody? How could they?" she said faintly as she got up and walked to the door.

"Thanks, Nikole," Curtis told her as he folded his laptop closed.

"You're welcome. Anytime," Nikole said softly as she opened the door and stepped out into the hallway.

Chapter 8

After getting her mani-pedi, Nikole lounged around on the balcony of her suite until it was time for her to try her luck at the casinos. Every since she had left Curtis's suite that morning, she couldn't get him off of her mind. She wanted another Nuvo excuse for the intense attraction, but this time, she didn't have one.

In all of her years, Nikole had never experienced love or a relationship. She only saw herself as entertainment for money, and besides that, Block strictly forbid her from seeing any of the clients outside of her work. All of her days were filled with different men that she was paid to please.

This attraction to Curtis was foreign to Nikole, and she didn't know which way to go with it. Block had always kept her so tied up on dates that she never had the time to meet anyone on this level. This time out and about gave Nikole a feeling of freedom that she'd never experienced before, and she enjoyed it.

After touching herself up in the bathroom mirror, she grabbed her clutch bag and headed downstairs to the casino. Entering the MGM casino was like entering an amusement park full of money. As she walked by the blackjack and roulette tables, she noticed how everyone held some type of alcoholic beverage in one hand and passed around money freely with the other. After exchanging her cash for the casino currency, she found herself an empty seat at the slot machines. Before she could get comfortable, a slim, White, happy-go-lucky waitress was bringing her a complimentary drink on the house. Nikole gladly accepted the drink and then turned her attention back to the slot machine.

Three hours later, still sitting in the same spot, Nikole had lost over $1,000. Disgusted at her losses, she decided to call it a night. On her way up to her room, she picked up a specialty sub at the famous sandwich shop, Witchcraft, and headed for the elevator. As she waited for it to open, she heard her name being called.

"Nikole! Nikole!" Curtis called out as he hurried over to her.

"Hey, Curtis," she answered as he approached.

"Where are you headed?" he asked.

"Back to my ro0om. The slot machines just robbed me blind, so now I'm going to go pig out on this," Nikole said, holding the sandwich up for him to see.

"Look, it's still early, and evidently, you haven't eaten. How about you accompany me to Joël Robuchon tonight?" Curtis asked insistently.

"What am I going to do with this?" Nikole asked, holding up the bag with the sandwich.

Before she knew it, Curtis had grabbed the bag and tossed it into the trashcan by the elevator. "Come on," he said. "Let me show you how a woman of your stature is supposed to be dining in the city of Las Vegas." He grabbed her hand and led the way to Joël Robuchon.

"But we don't have reservations," Nikole protested as they entered the five-star restaurant known for its fine French cuisine.

"Just ride with me, ma'am," Curtis joked.

"Hello, Mr. Conway. We are delighted to have you tonight. Table for two, I suppose?" asked the *maitre 'd* as he led Curtis and Nikole to a secluded table in the far corner of the restaurant. "Just summon me when you are ready to place your order, sir. I'll be up front," he said as he walked off.

"I told you I got you. Just believe in me." Curtis told Nikole as they looked over the menu.

"Oh, I totally forgot I'm with the famous author everybody seems to know but me," Nikole laughed.

"You are going to get to know me real well. I promise you that," Curtis said assuredly as he reached over and touched her hand.

Nikole had never been in this type of situation and really didn't know how to take Curtis. She was so used to the pay-and-play dating that she was totally out of touch with genuine relations. Nikole really wanted to do what was right, if only she knew which way to go. After pondering her next move, she decided to just give up and follow his lead.

"I really do enjoy your company, but I just can't understand why a woman such as yourself isn't already taken," Curtis stated as he brought his wine glass to his lips to take a sip.

"I'm just too busy. It's... it's... it's just hard to explain." Nikole paused, trying hard not to reveal what her life truly consisted of, but at the same time wanting to tell Curtis the truth.

"Would it be a problem if I wanted to see more of you?" Curtis asked as he gazed into her eyes.

"No... no... not a problem at all. I would really like that," Nikole responded, returning his gaze and leaning into him.

Their eyes never wandered, and their gaze didn't disconnect, even when their lips met for a soft, breathtaking kiss. Nikole had never known what it felt like to kiss a man of her own free will, but now she knew and wanted more.

Chapter 9

Back in Atlanta, Block and Bella were busy scheduling dates for Nikole and the rest of the girls for the big week. Tuesday and Wednesday were the busiest days of the big annual convention that would bring all of Block's wealthiest clients to the city. Block and Bella had taken the initiative to go ahead and schedule all the dates beforehand.

Block was not surprised to see that a majority of his clients had requested Nikole. She was in demand to the point where they were forced to turn clients away, which was totally against Block's principles, considering to him, all money was good money. After checking all the accounts of clients who were requesting Nikole, he made her available only to the wealthiest, highest-paying clients. Block also made a mental note to go out and scout for new clients that week.

Ring! Ring! Ring!

"Hello?" Block answered as he flipped through his Rolodex looking for Tim Kaplan, the CEO of World Mobile Communications so he could confirm the date he had arranged for him this week.

"Hey, my friend! How are you?" asked Jose Santana, head of one of the most prominent drug cartels on the west coast.

Jose and Block went way back. Block had met Jose through Shantea, one of his first girls. Shantea was the one who convinced Block to leave the streets and start a call-girl service. At first, Block was reluctant, but after seeing all of the money in the call-girl hustle, he tried it and became a rich man. In return, Block rewarded Shantea with riches beyond her wildest dreams, but it wasn't enough for her. One night, two masked men kicked in Block's door and robbed him of close to a million dollars in cash and valuables. The masked men held him at gunpoint and demanded he open his floor safe. Block knew right then who was behind the robbery, because the only person who knew of his floor safe was Shantea. A week later, Shantea was found dead, naked, with her hands and legs bound, in a car that had been doused with gasoline and set on fire. The case was filed with Atlanta police as an unsolved murder.

"What's going on, Jose?" Block asked, hoping he was throwing another one of his big orgies and needed about ten girls.

"I need a girl who can drive," Jose said.

Block knew exactly what he meant. Every couple of months, a big shipment came in for Jose, and he needed a girl to drive it out to his distributor. Block always handpicked one of his White girls with a valid driver's license for the job, and Jose always paid Block handsomely for the girl to make the drive.

"I got you, my friend. When do you need her?" Block asked as he thought of a girl for the job.

"Tomorrow at five. Have her come down to the shop on Campbelton to pick the car up," Jose instructed.

"Okay. No problem."

"Thanks, my friend."

"Anytime," Block replied and hung up.

"Everything is in order," Bella announced, entering the room and walking over to Block's desk. "Got to be Jose," Bella said, looking at the note Block had written to himself about the driver and a valid license.

Block made sure he filled Bella in on every aspect of the business just in case he could not be there for some reason. Bella had shown years ago how loyal she was to Block. At one time, Block almost fell weak and thought about inviting Bella into his bedroom, which was totally against his rule of never sleeping with the help. Over time, they became the best of friends. Block had retired her years ago after seeing she had such a mind for business and her hustle. He brought her in to help manage the girls and school them on the game, from proper etiquette to making clients pay for additional services. Bella was a vital piece to all of Block's success.

"You right. Yeah, Jose needs a driver, which we will gladly accommodate him with," Block said, smiling as he thought about the easy ten grand he was going to make for the trip.

"Yes we will," Bella chimed in, smiling at him.

"Everything set?" Block asked.

"Yeah. Everything is a go. All of the dates are logged in. We looking at about 900 grand, and that's just for two days."

"That's what I'm talkin' about! Damn, the price of pussy is music to my ears!" Block screamed as he leaned back in his oversized leather desk chair and put his feet on the desk.

"While checking the books over, I noticed most of that is going to be coming from Nikole. I don't know what that girl is doing, but they sure don't mind paying the price for her company."

"How much is she generating?" Block asked curiously.

"Just put it like this... she's bringing in more than half of the 900 grand."

"Yeah!" Block spat.

"That shouldn't surprise you because just this year, she's brought in over a million. These foreigners love her ass... literally!" Bella barked.

"Damn! I knew she was knocking down numbers, but I didn't know she was bringing in that much."

"Yeah, she's our franchise player," Bella joked.

"Well, I guess the trip to Vegas was well worth it," Block said as he laid his head back and looked up at the rotating ceiling fan and thought about all the money Nikole was going to make him that week and in the upcoming year.

Chapter 10

"So, it's the female that does the hunting while the male sits around waiting to eat. That's what's up," Curtis joked as he and Nikole strolled hand in hand through the lion habitat at the MGM grand.

"Yeah. Typical male," Nikole laughed.

"Hey! Low blow!" Curtis snapped back.

"Oh? Is somebody touched by my declaration of the truth?" Nikole asked as she linked her arm into his.

"I just want to show you different from the typical male," Curtis said softly as he stopped, grabbed her around the waist, and pulled her close to him.

"I'd like that," Nikole responded as he took her into his arms and gently kissed her.

After being educated on lions and checking out the different lion showcases, they decided to skip the David Copperfield show at the MGM Garden Arena for a nightcap and a movie. As they walked through the hotel lobby and headed back up to Curtis's suite, they stopped and turned when they heard Nikole's name being called from behind them.

"Nekoal! Nekoal!" screamed a drunken African gentleman in a two-piece suit and some oversized shades.

Nikole was at a loss for words as Abar, the owner of several exotic car dealerships and a frequent client of hers, approached them. Nikole prayed he wouldn't say the wrong thing and expose her in front of Curtis.

"You know him?" Curtis asked as Abar continued in their direction.

Before Nikole could answer, Abar was up in their faces, reeking of alcohol. "Nikole, how are you? Good to see you!" he slurred as he tightly held a plastic cup.

"Hi," Nikole responded nervously.

"Oh! I'm sorry for being rude. My name is Abar." He apologized and extended his hand to Curtis.

"No problem. My name is Curtis," he answered, shaking the man's hand.

"Hi, Abar. I didn't recognize you behind those big shades," Nikole said as she flashed a phony smile.

"I've been just fine. Matter of fact, I spoke with Block about you not too long ago, and he told me—"

"Sorry, Abar, but we are in a bit of a rush. I will make sure I tell Block I saw you," Nikole said, cutting him off.

"Okay, okay. Tell Block I—"

"Take it easy, Abar," Nikole said firmly as she grabbed Curtis's hand and pulled him to the elevator in a hurry, leaving Abar standing in the middle of the lobby with his cup in hand and a confused look on his face.

"Sorry about that, Curtis. My old friend Abar can get real long winded after a couple of drinks," she explained.

"No need to apologize. We all have at least one

friend like that in the bunch," Curtis replied as they waited for the elevator.

Nikole was relieved to be away from Abar and behind the closed doors of the elevator. Exiting the elevator, they walked and hugged all the way to Curtis's suite.

"One more week of signings, and then it's back to home sweet home," Curtis said as they entered his suite.

"I really wish I could say the same. My last day is tomorrow," Nikole said sadly.

"So, you just going to leave me here all by myself," Curtis spat playfully.

"It looks that way," Nikole reluctantly said as she plopped down on the leather sofa in front of the forty-inch wall-mounted flat-screen TV.

"Can I make a suggestion?" Curtis asked, sitting next to her.

"What's up?" Nikole asked, turning to face him.

"How about you stay with me for the rest of the week?" Curtis asked, putting his arm around her.

"What about work? I will surely be fired," she responded, thinking about Block and hoping Curtis wouldn't inquire about her occupation.

"Nikole, I really like you and enjoy your company, so I'm willing to do whatever it takes to keep you here with me," Curtis said firmly.

"Curtis, I just… I just can't. I will be fired, and I really need my job."

"So call in sick."

"I… I can't."

"Nikole, I am willing to pay all of your bills from here on out until you find another job if you get fired for calling in sick," Curtis assured her.

"Curtis, I…" she started. She thought about Block and the convention, and then she thought about the unhappy, miserable life she was living. "Okay, Curtis. I will stay, but if I get fired, I'm becoming your dependent," Nikole called out, glad she had brought extra clothes.

"I'd love that. I'd enjoy taking care of you as my own," Curtis said as he started to plant soft kisses on her neck.

Things were moving fast for Nikole. She didn't know what to do about her new feelings. She badly wanted to take things further with Curtis, but she wondered what Block would think, what he would do. She knew she would definitely have to stop working for Block if she and Curtis got serious. After contemplating the situation thoroughly, she decided to just live in the moment. Enjoying the feel of Curtis's soft kisses, she closed her eyes and let him take over her whole body.

Chapter 11

"Oh yes, Curtis!" Nikole screamed as Curtis buried his hardness deep inside of her. She tightly gripped the arm of the leather sofa while Curtis slid in and out of her wetness. "Oh yes, baby! Oh! Ooh! Ooh! Yes!" Nikole purred.

"Shit, Nikole! Ah yeah! Ohh! Yeah!" Curtis barked as he dug deeper and deeper.

"Baby, I'm about to… cum!" Nikole screamed as Curtis long-stroked her, rubbing his manhood up against her G-spot.

"Give it to me, baby! Oh… I'm coming! Ahhh!" Curtis screamed.

"Ohh! Yes! Yes! Yes!" Nikole yelled out in

ecstasy.

"Ahhh!" Curtis moaned as he released his juices into an accepting Nikole.

They laid in each other's arms, naked and speechless, until they both passed out.

The next morning, the ringing of Nikole's cell phone woke her up. *Ring! Ring! Ring!* "Yeah?" Nikole answered groggily.

"Hey, baby girl. What time should I be expecting you?" Block asked, catching her off guard.

"Oh… uh…" Nikole stuttered.

"You okay?" Block asked in a concerned tone.

"Yeah, I'm good. I was asleep. Give me a few minutes to fully wake up, and I'll call you right back," Nikole said awkwardly, needing some time to come up with a good excuse for making plans to stay for an extra week.

"No need. Just let me know what time you'll be arriving in town, because I got you scheduled for a date tonight with Harvey Wince, the real estate magnate. I told him all about you, and he's anxiously waiting to meet you," Block told her excitedly, thinking of the couple thousand he had already charged to the man's account.

"Uh, okay... about... uh, three, I guess. I'll call you then," Nikole lied, thinking about his reaction when she didn't show up.

"Good time, baby girl. I'll see you then. Oh, one more thing... you have a long list of clients for this week, and I'm placing some extra money in your account."

"Oh. There ain't no need to—"

"I will deposit more next week, and Bella told me to tell you she picked you up a couple of new outfits for this week also," Block interrupted.

"Tell her I said I appreciate it," Nikole told him dryly as she looked over at a still-sleeping Curtis.

"Go on back to sleep. I'll see you later today, baby girl," Block said and ended the call.

Nikole sat on the edge of the sofa, naked, with phone in hand. She was lost in thought. For a moment, she considered just leaving, but her newfound feelings for Curtis wouldn't allow it. Dismissing the thought, she lay back down on Curtis.

A few hours later, they were up and making plans to go to the Crazy Horse to watch the female dancers move to the rhythm under the night glow lights, sexually portraying the female form as an art. Before they left, Nikole packed up all of her belongings out of her suite and moved into Curtis's.

"You about ready in there?" Curtis called out to Nikole in the bathroom.

"One minute!" Nikole yelled out as she turned around and double-checked herself in the wall mirror.

"Show starts at four!" Curtis called.

"Okay, okay!" Nikole pouted jokingly as she opened the bathroom door.

"Beautiful," Curtis cooed, admiring Nikole, who was standing before him in a bright red Cavalli ensemble that tastefully accentuated her perfect shape.

"Thanks," Nikole said, starting to blush.

Beep! Beep! Beep! The ringing of Nikole's cell phone reminded her of her earlier conversation with Block. Picking her cell phone up off the table, she saw that it was Block and quickly pressed 'Ignore.'

"Your job?" Curtis inquired after seeing her ignore the call.

"Yeah. They're probably writing up my termination papers as we speak," Nikole lied, thinking about how mad Block was going to be when she didn't show up.

"Don't worry. I'll take care of you," Curtis assured her as he walked over and took her into his strong arms.

"You better," Nikole said, half-jokingly, thinking about Block.

Chapter 12

As the week rolled on, Nikole and Curtis got to know each other in every way. Nikole accompanied him to all of his book signings and began to realize how famous he really was. Every night after the book signings, they retreated back to the suite and made love until they passed out.

"Is there such a thing as love at first sight?" Curtis asked Nikole as they cuddled naked in the king-sized bed.

"I was thinking the same thing. I think it is... yes there is," Nikole told him as she laid her head on his broad chest.

"Nikole, I want you to know I am a man that does whatever it takes to get what I want. Being with you this week has been a real pleasure, and I would hate for it to end here... or ever."

"Ahh, Curtis," Nikole smiled.

"I want you to come home with me and let me take care of you like the queen you are," Curtis added while rubbing his hands through Nikole's hair.

"Oh, Curtis, I just... I can't just..." she stammered, at a loss for words.

"Nikole, I want you to marry me."

Nikole's heart skipped a beat. She used to laugh at all of the silly women who married men not long after meeting them, but now she was in the same situation. Whirlwind romances and instant marriages are common in Vegas, and Nikole didn't want to fall victim to the Vegas tradition, but at the same time, she wanted to be with Curtis in every way. "Curtis... are you sure this is what you want?"

"I asked you if there is such thing as love at first sight."

"I just don't want us to do the wrong thing," Nikole said softly.

"You not feeling what I'm feeling?" Curtis asked.

"Oh no, it's not that. It's just—" Nikole started

"Nikole, just go with what you feel. Life is short, and we have to learn to live a little. Every split-second decision isn't a bad one or a wrong one. Just go with your feelings," Curtis chimed in, cutting her off.

"Yes," Nikole whispered as she lifted her head up off his chest and passionately kissed him.

They made love until they passed out again in each other's arms.

The next morning, it was time for them to check out. Nikole gathered all of her things and packed them in her suitcase. Grabbing her phone and sticking it in her purse, she cringed at the thought of ignoring Block's calls all week. She knew he was beyond furious and frantically looking for her.

"What time does your flight leave?" Nikole asked Curtis as he packed up all of his books and clothes.

"At four. I have a few people to meet with before I leave. What time is your flight?"

"One o'clock," Nikole replied as she pulled her rolling luggage to the door.

"I will call you when I get in town," Curtis said, wrapping his arms around her waist.

"Okay," Nikole said softly as they kissed like it was their last.

"Need me to walk you down?" Curtis asked, still holding Nikole in his arms.

"Nah. I'm a big girl. You go ahead and finish packing," Nikole told him, stepping away and opening the door.

"I love you, Nikole," Curtis declared.

"Love you too," Nikole replied faintly as she stepped out with her Gucci luggage in tow.

Locking the door behind Nikole, Curtis hurriedly went and dug a black leather pouch out of his canvas bag. Emptying its contents on the bed, he tore the white rocks out of the plastic they were wrapped in. He picked up the glass pipe and wedged the small white rock in the tip shakily. Fishing through the contents scattered on the bed, he picked out a lighter. He brought the glass pipe to his lips and flicked his lighter and guided the flame to the tip with the wedged white rock. He pulled the smoke until it filled his lungs. His eyes rolled back into his head, and his lips twisted as he exhaled. Five minutes later, he had wedged his last rock in the pipe. He looked around the room, bug-eyed and his lips twisted, desperately wanting another hit.

Chapter 13

Arriving back in Atlanta, Nikole was suddenly thrust back into reality. She turned into her neighborhood and admired all the nice palatial homes that lined the streets. She thought about how far she had come since the rooming house.

She pulled her Aston Martin into the garage and unloaded her luggage. Walking into the house, Nikole was shocked to see that someone had been there. Her fifty-inch plasma TV was on, and an empty Corona beer bottle was on the table next to the couch. She knew then that it could only be Block; he was the only one with a key. Nikole knew he was probably looking for her, and her heart raced as she thought of not returning his calls and not filling him in on her whereabouts.

Lost in thought, Nikole headed up to her bedroom with her luggage. Looking around, she noticed Block had been through her room. He had left her drawers open and her closet light on. Becoming furious at his intrusion, Nikole picked up her cell phone and dialed his number. When he didn't answer, she left him a message to call her ASAP.

After unpacking her bags, she picked up the phone and called Curtis to let him know she had made it home. His voicemail came on after the third ring, so she hung up without leaving a message.

Finally, after getting everything situated, Nikole went into the bathroom and ran some bath water. She stripped out of her clothes while the water filled her tub. A few minutes later, she was submerged in the warm water, listening to Sade sing on the bathroom MP3 player. She closed her eyes and dozed off.

Slap! Slap! Splash!

Nikole was suddenly awakened by a slap from Block, who stood over her in the tub.

"Ah! Block!" Nikole screamed out in panic.

"Bitch! You must think I'm something to play with! I saved your bitch ass, and this is how you repay me?"

"Block! Please! Just—"

Slap! Slap! Block reached over and slapped Nikole twice more as she cowered in the far corner of the tub. Reaching over, he grabbed her by the hair and pulled her roughly up out of the tub, exposing her nakedness. "Bitch! You didn't even have enough respect to answer my calls! I bring you out of the ghetto, put you in this nice house, a nice ride, and you just tell me to fuck off? I lost over a quarter-mill this week banking on your punk ass!" *Slap! Slap!*

Nikole fell to the bathroom floor, squirming around like a fish out of water, trying to get away from Block.

"Block, please just stop! Let me explain! I did call, but—"

Slap! Slap! Slap! The more Nikole tried to talk, the madder Block became. After his third slap, Nikole bolted for the door with Block hot on her heels.

"Please, Block! Stop!" Nikole yelled out as she

ran through her bedroom, trying to get away from Block, who was only a couple of steps behind her.

Before she could reach her bedroom door, Block had scooped her up and slammed her to the floor.

"Block! I called! I swear! Block, please!" Nikole cried as Block stood over her.

"Let me tell you something. I made you, you trifling-ass bitch! The position you in now, I put you in, but instead of thanking me and staying loyal, you lie and say 'Fuck you!' Well, now, since you don't give a fuck about the person that took you in and made you very wealthy, I'll just take it all back! Get your shit and get out of MY house and leave MY car in the garage! I want every piece of clothing MY money paid for! Now you're free to go and do what you want, bitch!"

Slap! Block slapped Nikole one last time as he walked away, leaving her crying on the floor, naked.

Nikole had never prepared for this day. She knew when Block purchased the house and car in his name, it would one day come to this, but she planned on being prepared. Now, she was without a car and homeless, but at least she was free from Block's demands. All she could think of was Curtis and his invitation of marriage, which she was now glad she had accepted.

"By the way, I left your account with what you came in with—nothing! Be out of my shit by the time I get back!" Block yelled from downstairs as he exited out the front door.

Nikole peeked out of the window and watched Block climb into his black-on-black Denali and drive off. She hurriedly packed up some clothes and called Curtis. There was still no answer, so she decided to call a cab and get a hotel room until Curtis arrived back in town. While waiting on the cab, Nikole counted the money she had stashed away. Counting the money a second time, she knew the $17,000 would be enough to live off of for a while. She packed the money away and went into the bathroom to look in the mirror. Relieved that her face was still in tact from Block's brutal assault, she packed up all she could carry.

As she looked around at her beautiful home, tears welled up in her eyes. "Fuck Block!" she said to herself as she went down to the garage and grabbed a can of gasoline. She poured gas all over the Aston Martin and walked through the house, drenching the expensive carpet.

A few minutes later, her cab was pulling up. *Honk! Honk!*

Nikole peeked out of the blinds and saw the cab out front. She grabbed her bags and headed for the door. As she stood just outside the doorway with her oversized Chanel shades on, she lit a match, tossed it back into the house and hurrily got in the cab. Before the cab had turned the corner, she could see the black smoke filling the air.

Chapter 14

Nikole checked into a hotel for the night, hoping Curtis would arrive back in town soon. She knew that by now, Block had been contacted by the police about the fire at his home. She also knew he was on a rampage, desperately trying to find her to unleash is wrath.

Nikole planned on burying her past and starting a new life with Curtis. As she lay in the hotel bed, she contemplated how she was going to explain her homelessness and lack of transportation to Curtis. Going over different explanations, she disregarded the thoughts and dozed off into a deep sleep.

Beep! Beep! Beep!

Nikole was suddenly awakened by the beeping of her cell phone. Looking at the screen, she saw that it was Curtis. "Hello?" she hastily answered, trying to hide her excitement.

"Hey, baby!" Curtis replied with enthusiasm.

"How was your flight back?" Nikole asked.

"Baby, you wouldn't believe it. I missed my flight. I had my times mixed up. I'm just now about to leave."

"Sorry to hear that, baby. I thought you was already back," Nikole said, disappointed.

"My flight is boarding in ten minutes. I'll be home in no time. Can you pick me up from the airport?"

Nikole was caught off guard by his request. "Yeah. What time are you arriving?"

"I'll be around five. Is that okay?"

"Oh yeah, no problem. I'll be there," Nikole stammered while thinking of a way to get some immediate transportation.

"See you then. Love you, Nikki," Curtis said with passion and sincerity.

"Love you, too, Curtis," Nikole replied, hanging up the phone.

After Googling rental agencies, Nikole found three nearby locations. At five o'clock, she parked out front of the airport in a rented Lincoln Town Car. Upon seeing Curtis coming out through the exit doors, she stepped out of the car and waved her hand in the air as she called out his name.

He quickly spotted Nikole and hastily made his way over to the car with his luggage. "Home sweet home," Curtis exclaimed as he grabbed Nikole into his arms and kissed her passionately.

"Mmmm," Nikole uttered as she tightened her grip around Curtis's neck.

Nikole felt a sense of security in Curtis's arms. She was in a safe place now, for Curtis was her knight in shining armor.

"Let's get going before Officer Friendly back there gives us a ticket," Curtis said, releasing Nikole as the airport police headed in their direction.

Nikole got behind the wheel of the Town Car and followed Curtis's directions to his place. As they rode down 285, they talked about the good times they had enjoyed in Vegas and their future together.

Curtis said the words Nikole had prayed for all

day. "I want you to move in with me, Nikole."

Nikole hesitated before she answered, even though she knew she would say *yes*. "Are you sure you want that, Curtis?" Nikole asked as he directed her to turn on the next block.

"I am positive, baby," Curtis said as they turned into a gated community on the outskirts of Atlanta.

As Nikole navigated the rented Lincoln through the tree-lined streets, she was amazed at the multimillion-dollar homes that were separated by acres and acres of beautifully manicured lawns.

"Right there," said Curtis, pointing.

Nikole couldn't believe her eyes. The house had to be valued in the high seven-figure range. As she pulled up in front of the big iron gates that separated the house from the street, Curtis handed her his gate key, which she inserted into the gold box positioned right outside the car window. When she removed the key, the big iron gates creaked open.

Driving through the gates, Nikole was surrounded by statues of medieval goddesses and a roaring fountain. When she pulled up to the house, she caught a glimpse of an Olympic-sized swimming pool with a connected Jacuzzi in the back yard next to a tennis court. Nikole knew she would be the queen of this castle... and soon. "Your home is beautiful, Curtis," she told him as they pulled under the six-car garage next to a Maybach.

"*Our* home," Curtis corrected as he leaned over and kissed Nikole softly on the lips.

Nikole wanted to pinch herself. She couldn't believe her good fortune. She was now free from Block's reins and about to become Mrs. Curtis Conway. She helped him gather his bags and headed into the house.

Her heart skipped a beat as she entered the lavish home that was about to be hers. She was amazed at the size of the dimly lit crystal chandelier that hung above the white and gold grand piano. As she walked through the foyer, she tried to catch her reflection off the shiny marble floor. This house was something beyond Nikole's wildest dreams. Making her way to the living quarters, she passed a gigantic in-the-wall fish tank that was home to the biggest, most colorful fish she had ever seen.

"Are you okay?" Curtis asked as they made their

way to his bedroom with his luggage.

"Yeah, I'm fine—just admiring your beautiful home."

"*Our* home!" Curtis corrected, this time with emphasis.

"Sorry. I just keep forgetting," Nikole mumbled.

"Get used to it, Nikki." Curtis smiled as he opened the heavy wooden door to his bedroom and stepped to the side so Nikole could enter.

Nikole almost fainted when she walked in. She was surprised to see that Curtis had ceiling-to-floor mirrors, a wet bar, and a Jacuzzi in his bedroom. The king-sized cherry oak bed looked like a twin-sized in the spacious bedroom. A seventy-two-inch flat-screen TV hung on the wall in front of the bed. Looking across the room, Nikole saw a bathroom that was the size of her previous bedroom. Nikole walked over to Curtis's custom-built work desk that sat in a far corner. It held an expensive computer system that he used for writing his masterpieces.

"How do you like your new room?" Curtis asked as he sat his bags down in the corner.

"It's...wonderful," Nikole answered hesitantly,

trying to picture herself really living in the beautiful home.

"I will get the movers to help you gather your things tomorrow if that's okay with you," Curtis offered.

"That's fine, but I don't really have much, and besides, most of my stuff wouldn't go well in this house anyway," Nikole declared as she surveyed the immaculate room again.

"Well, just get your necessary items and donate the rest," Curtis advised as he pulled the plush curtains back to let the sunshine bathe the room.

Nikole thought about the few things she had in the hotel room. She made a mental note to go shopping and to go to a car lot to get some reliable transportation. She knew that, in due time, Curtis would see to her needs. Right then and there, Nikole told herself she would not allow her past to affect her future.

"I cannot wait to make you Mrs. Conway," Curtis whispered in Nikole's ear as he embraced his wife-to-be.

"I can't wait to be Mrs. Conway," Nikole said

faintly, thinking of how her new life would be.

"You are so beautiful," Curtis said as he nibbled on Nikole's neck.

Nikole blushed as Curtis kissed her and placed his hands under her shirt. A few minutes later, they were in bed making passionate love.

Chapter 15

"I can't believe this bitch burned my house down!" Block screamed as he and Bella stood outside the burnt-down palatial home he had purchased for Nikole. "The bitch could have at least spared the Aston!" Block spat as they turned to walk away.

Bella knew Block was very calculating and vindictive, and she was sure he was plotting revenge. "I just can't believe Nikole would do something so drastic like this after all we have done for her," Bella snapped as she climbed into the driver seat of her 600 Mercedes Benz.

"Ungrateful bitch," Block said in a calm,

menacing tone as he pulled his cell phone from his jacket pocket.

"Where is she now?" Bella asked as she put the car in 'Drive' and pressed a heavy foot on the accelerator.

"That's just what I'm about to find out. She will not get away with this bullshit," Block added as he dialed several numbers for his police department contact.

"Hello. Atlanta police department. Can I help you?" a young female voice asked from the other end.

"Yeah. Is Captain Adams in?" Block asked in an urgent tone.

"Yes he is. May I ask who's calling?" the young voice inquired.

"Tell him it's Brian Block from narcotics," Block responded in an official tone.

"Narcotics?" the female asked, confused. She was in narcotics and had never heard of anyone named 'Block.'

"Yeah. DeKalb County narcotics."

"Oh, okay!" she replied and hastily paged the

captain.

When she got Captain Adams on the line and relayed Block's message, he hurried her off the phone and picked up on Line Three, where Block was patiently waiting. "Block, my brotha! How's it going?" Captain Adams asked in a friendly but agitated tone.

Block really despised Captain Adams, even though he was a high-paying client. Captain Adams always tried to use his position with Block to get free dates, which Block would never tolerate. Block hated the police, but he despised Captain Adams as a man as well. The captain could not be trusted by any means. Block hated that he knew of his operation and planned to eliminate him on the right day, but for now, he had to play the part. "I need your help, good friend," Block said. "I need to locate one of my girls who's gone missing."

"Missing or run away?" Captain Adams asked sarcastically.

"Missing!" Block said again, this time heatedly.

"No problem. Give me everything you have on her."

Block described Nikole from her light brown eyes to the tattoo of a black butterfly that was wrapped around her ankle.

"I will put the word out in all departments and also assign one of my best men to the case," Captain Adams assured Block.

"I appreciate that, Captain, and after she is found, I will reward you handsomely and treat you to the girl of your choice, on the house," Block told him, hating his own words. Block could see the fat, Black Danny Glover lookalike smiling from ear to ear.

"That's a ten-four, brother. We will find her, and since you're in a generous mood, how about booking me a date tonight on the house, just for good business?" Captain Adams added.

Block knew this was more of a condition of him finding Nikole than a simple request, so he agreed. Block wanted to tell the captain to fuck off, but he decided against it because he knew if anyone could find Nikole, the captain could. "No problem," he said grudgingly. "Just call me later with your request," Block told him through clenched teeth.

"Will do, brother. Now that's what I call good

business."

"Later!" Block yelled as he pressed the 'End' button on his cell phone. "This bitch is going to pay as soon as I find her ass. I'm going to make it my business to put that no-good bitch right back on them rooming house steps where I took her from!" Block barked as he put his cell phone back into his jacket pocket.

"Man, Nikole knows better," Bella said, slapping the steering wheel, hating what Nikole had done. Bella loved Nikole like a daughter and didn't want to see any harm come to her, but now she had crossed Block, the one person Bella couldn't protect her from. Bella knew Block wouldn't rest until he found her, and when he did, she knew he would punish the girl severely. Deep down, Bella hoped and prayed Block would never find Nikole.

They both sat in silence as they headed out to Bella's downtown loft, where Block's truck awaited them.

Chapter 16

Six Months Later

"Girl, put that thing away. It's blinding me!" China laughed, taking a closer look a the ten-carat diamond ring Curtis gave Nikole on their wedding day.

"Oh stop it, girl," Nikole said humbly as they made their way into the BMW dealership.

Nikole was still in hiding from Block. She had run into China in the mall a few weeks after her wedding day. She had told China of her and Block's situation, and China promised she would never reveal her whereabouts to Block. Since that day, she and China had been in contact on a regular basis.

China also confided in Nikole about wanting to leave Block's escort service, but she was scared of what Block would do.

"That's the one right there, girl!" China called out, pointing to a cherry red BMW 760 Li with all-black interior.

"Oh yeah, I like that one too! Excuse me, mister!" Nikole called out to the slightly balding Italian sales-man.

Thirty minutes later, Nikole was pulling out of the dealership in the BMW while China followed her in her late-model Infiniti. They arrived back at Nikole's place forty-five minutes later.

"Girl, I appreciate you taking me car shopping today. Curtis is just going to love this car," Nikole told China as they sat in the TV room watching soaps.

"Girl, you are so lucky. It's like a dream come true. You have it all... a good—not to mention rich—husband who showers you with expensive gifts, a beautiful home, and to top it off, you're expecting a beautiful little girl. Nikole, I am so happy for you," China said faintly through watery eyes.

"Oh thank you, sis," Nikole replied softly,

reaching over to give China a sisterly hug.

"I want to live again," China said through sniffs, hugging Nikole.

"Like I told you earlier, you can come live here, and I will look out for you until you get situated. You can stay in the guest house and drive one of Curtis's cars. I promise you will be totally safe here. Block's connections don't run this far out. Girl, this is a totally different world. I have so many wonderful new friends, and if you decide to move in, you will too. On top of that, Curtis has got a lot of rich, handsome, single friends," Nikole said with a wink.

"I just don't want to be a burden," China said, wiping her eyes.

"Look, China… we go way back. You are like a sister to me, and I know firsthand what you are going through. I promise you that it won't be a problem at all," Nikole assured her.

"You sure?" China asked faintly.

"Positive. Now, go get your stuff and come on!" Nikole insisted.

When China moved in, Curtis was out of town on a book signing tour. When he arrived home, he was really pleased with the new addition to the household. Nikole had introduced China as a friend from high school that was trying to get away from an abusive boyfriend. They had made a pat never to reveal their past lives to Curtis or anyone else in their new social circle.

In no time, China became like part of the family. When she had first met Curtis, her heart skipped a beat. She was instantly attracted to the fine, rich, famous man. Her loyalty to Nikole overrode her initial attraction. She refused to let a man come in between her and Nikole's bond.

On the other hand, Curtis lusted after China day in and day out. When he first met Nikole, he felt like she was the most beautiful woman in the world—until he met the green-eyed, half-Black, half-Chinese China. China had caught him watching her on several occasions but always acted as if she didn't notice.

China also noticed how Curtis often buried himself in his home office and later came out with his mouth twitching and his eyes bugged out. She asked Nikole one day if Curtis had some kind of medical condition that made him that way, and Nikole told her she noticed it soon after they were married. He had explained to Nikole that sitting in front of his computer screen for a long time straining his brain and his eyes had that effect on him. Nikole took his admissions as true and never asked about it again, so Curtis had no reason to tell his trusting wife anything about the glass pipe and the rocked-up cocaine.

China's life had been drastically changed. She was now courted by some of the wealthiest men in the city. She was wined and dined at some of the most elegant restaurants. She was introduced to Curtis's best friend, Todd, at a social gathering for one of Curtis's books, and ever since that night, they had been going steady. Todd was a publicist for some of the biggest names in the business.

Everything in Nikole and China's world was perfect. Block was a past memory to both of them. After China didn't make a date Block had set up for her with one of his highest-paying clients, he became worried. He called her and went to her home on several occasions to see what was going on. After his last visit to her home, he saw she had run off, just like Nikole. Looking through the back bedroom window, he saw open, empty drawers and closets.

He angrily made his way back to his truck and dialed Bella's cell number. He told her to call and check China's bank balance. A few minutes later, while speeding back to his house, he received a call from Bella, letting him know the account had been emptied and closed. Block was now furious; the thing he hated most was disloyalty. Still not able to locate Nikole and now having to track China down too, he was even angrier. He vowed to himself that both of them would pay for their betrayal.

Block was a man who was used to order and control, but now these two women had disrupted his whole household. The other girls were finding out about Nikole's and China's actions and starting to become disloyal and disrespectful. Block knew he had to get order back in his house if he was going to keep his business going.

The following weekend, Block called all the girls over for a mandatory meeting and demanded everyone attend. As the girls gathered around in Block's game room, they whispered amongst each other concerning the urgency of the meeting and what it could be about. Once Block made sure all the girls were accounted for, he entered the game room and locked the door behind him.

Singling out the disloyal, disrespectful girls, he moved them to the center of the room, where he chastised them severely one by one as the other girls stood by, looking on in shock and disbelief. Block wanted to show every girl he employed that loyalty and respect was a must. He wanted to make sure they knew he was in total control and that he would not tolerate any actions that went against his rules.

By the time he was finished, two of the girls needed medical attention, and Block told Bella to contact his on-call doctor, who immediately came over and administered proper care. From that day on, Block never had any more problems out of the girls.

Chapter 17

Block called Captain Adams every week for an update, but no one had heard from or seen Nikole for months. Block had even hired a private investigator to find Nikole, but he couldn't locate her either. Block had almost given up hope of finding Nikole when Bella burst into the room.

"She's been spotted!" Bella announced, causing Block to knock over his coffee and instantly stand behind his desk. "China's been spotted in her old neighborhood, visiting her gang-banging brother."

"Oh yeah?" Block responded faintly, hoping it would be news of Nikole. Overall, though, it was good news to him, and he would be happy to take care of at least one of the disloyal bitches. "Give me the address, and I'll take it from here," he told Bella as he picked up the phone from his desk.

A few minutes later, two heavily armed men were headed out to China's brother's apartment in the Greenbriar Mall area of Atlanta. As they pulled up in front of the apartment, they double-checked the door number against the number on the small strip of paper they were given. They shut off the engine of the old beat-up Chevy and casually headed to Apartment 209. Just as they were about to knock, they noticed the door was already ajar. Before entering the apartment, they pulled their guns and put on ski masks. Seeing no signs of life in the front room, they moved through the apartment with caution. Before they reached the kitchen, a lanky young boy with braids, talking on a cell phone, walked straight into their path. The boy was totally caught off guard by the two men, who instantly rushed him. As they pinned him to the ground, they inquired about China's location.

"Hey, man, I swear, I don't know nothing!" the lanky boy screamed as the two hulking men in ski masks and all black held him down with a gun pointed at his nose.

"Where is China?" one of the masked men asked again in a calm voice.

"Man, I don't—"

Before the boy could answer, the pistol connected with the side of his face, breaking his jaw. "I'm going to ask you again. Where is China?" the masked man demanded in a firm voice this time.

"Look here, lil buddy. Just tell us where China's at, and we're out of here, but as long as you play dumb, we're gonna keep punishing you," the second man snapped.

"Look, man, I don't—"

Slap! The second man slapped the young boy, causing severe pain to shoot down the side of his face.

"Wa... wait!" the boy slurred as blood trickled down the side of his mouth.

"Speak!" the first masked man barked.

"I... I... I can... call her," he said as his eyes began to water.

"Now we're getting somewhere," the first man

said, placing his gun back in his waistband.

The second masked man reached over and grabbed the boy's cell phone off the floor where it had landed next to his baseball cap. Both men watched in silence as he dialed his sister's number.

"Hello?" China answered on the second ring.

China loved her brother dearly. She had basically raised him when their grandmother died. They never knew their mother or father, who were both killed in a head-on collision by a drunk driver while the children were still in diapers. China took on motherly duties at the age of sixteen, when their grandmother became terminally ill and was bedridden for the next year. China took care of Chase up until he was old enough to take care of himself. Even though Chase was four years younger, he always referred to himself as 'the big brother.' At the age of eighteen, China met Block, and he made her a wealthy woman—at a cost.

"Sis, I need you to come over here," Chase said hesitantly, hoping China would pick up on his distress.

"Boy, what's up with you? You been smokin' that bad weed again? I'll be over later. I ain't forgot it's your birthday. I'll be over there around five," China spat playfully, thinking about the surprise she had for her little brother's birthday.

Chase instantly regretted making the phone call. He knew if these men hurt his sister, it would be all his fault. Chase promised to find out who was behind this and make them pay, whatever the cost.

The two masked men smiled behind their mask as they listened in. China was about to be hand delivered. The second gunman thought of what he was going to do with his half of the fifty grand they were being paid to bring China to Block.

The two men lifted Chase up off the floor and tied him up in a chair in the back room. After securing him and taping his mouth shut, they sat in silence as they waited for China to arrive.

A little after five, they heard a knock at the door, and then someone entered.

"Chase!" China called out as she made her way through the apartment.

The two men hastily made their way to the front of the apartment. As China reached the kitchen, the ski-masked men grabbed her and slammed her to

George Sherman Hudson

the floor. China's screams were muffled as one of
the men placed his gloved hand over her mouth.

Chapter 18

The two masked men had snatched her from her brother's apartment and dropped her off at an old abandoned warehouse in the back of a rundown strip mall in east Atlanta. Two hours later, Block and Bella walked into the dimly lit room.

"Well, well, well. What do we have here?" Block called out as he walked around China, who lay helplessly on the floor with her hands and ankles tied together in the cold, empty warehouse.

"Block, please don't hurt me," China pleaded weakly as she looked up from the hard cold floor at Block and Bella.

"Why shouldn't I?" Block asked calmly as he

bent down face to face with her.

"I... I... I don't know. I just wanted to be on my own. I was tired of selling myself. I—"

Slap! Block hit China so hard it caused her head to connect with the cold, hard cement. She cried out hysterically as Block delivered slap after slap to the side of her face. After tiring himself out, he reached down and untied her. "Get up, you nothing-ass bitch! I give you the world, and this is how you repay me?" Block screamed as China slowly rose to her feet.

"Block, please! I swear—"

Slap!

China fell back to the concrete, pleading with Block to have mercy on her.

Bella stood in the background, hoping Block would spare young China's life. Bella had raised and groomed a lot of the girls they employed, and over time, she began to see them as her daughters. She had once been in their position and could relate to their issues, but overall, her loyalty still rested with Block.

"Bella, give me your gun," Block ordered through clenched teeth.

Without saying a word, Bella reached into her

handbag and pulled out her nine-millimeter Glock and handed it to Block. Bella swore under her breath as Block cocked the gun back. She prayed he wouldn't use it.

"Get down on your knees!" Block ordered.

"Nooo! Block, please!" China cried as she reluctantly did as he said. She cried hysterically, begging and pleading Block not to kill her.

"Why shouldn't I kill you? You betrayed me, now give me one reason I should let you live!" Block yelled.

China swallowed hard before answering, "Because I know where Nikole is." She looked down at the drab gray cement, crying uncontrollably.

Block and Bella were surprised by her revelation. Block suddenly became excited at the news of Nikole's whereabouts. "What?" Block asked with enthusiasm.

"Where is she?" Bella chimed in, just as excited as Block.

"Are you going to let me live if I tell you?" China asked through sniffles.

"Well, I'll put it like this. If you don't tell us, you

won't walk out of here alive," Block said with a sneer.

"Block, plea—"

"Shut the fuck up and just tell me what you know about Nikole!" he screamed.

"Okay! Alright!" China cried.

China told Block and Bella everything she knew about Nikole's new life, right down to the floor plan of the house and the code to the security gate. Block smiled as China told them about Nikole's famous and wealthy husband. After hearing China out, Block pulled Bella to the side and told her of his intentions. Finding out that Nikole's husband had no idea of her past life, Block had a plan to make her pay.

After talking to Bella, Block moved his attention back to China. "I've come to the conclusion that I'll let you live, but you will help me carry out my plans," Block snapped.

"I can't hurt nobody. I told you everything I know. Please just let me go," China pleaded as she wiped tears from her eyes.

"Who's talking about hurting anybody? Plans have changed, and we're talking about money and getting paid," Block fired back.

China didn't know what Block's plans were, but to get out of the cold warehouse alive, she knew she had to agree. "Alright. What is it I have to do?" she asked faintly while wiping tears from her face with the back of her trembling hand.

"All I need you to do is supply me with all of Nikole's intentions after I give her my demands. I'm pretty sure she's going to confide in you after I make my contact. I want you to report to me daily on her every move. You're going to be my spy," Block said firmly.

"I can do—" China started.

"Don't forget how we found you the first time. You cross me again, and we will find you again, but next time, it won't end so nicely for you," Block said sincerely.

China knew Block had a lot of power and connections, so she made up her mind right then and there to help him carry out his plan, and then, hopefully, she would be free from his reins.

Block and Bella gave China specific instructions and went over their blackmail plan for the third time to make sure China fully understood their directions. After making sure she would be cooperative on every front, they exited the warehouse, leaving her standing in the middle of the floor, alone, wiping her tears.

Chapter 19

Getting out of the cab in front of her brother's apartment, China went in to make sure he was alright. After being grilled by him on the situation, she told him everything was cool and that it was all just a misunderstanding with an old hot-headed boyfriend. Bandaged and bruised, young Chase swore under his breath he would get revenge, whatever the cost, misunderstanding or not. After spending a little time with Chase, China gathered herself and headed home.

When she pulled into the driveway of Curtis and Nikole's home, she checked her face in the visor mirror. She pulled her hair down partially to cover the light bruise Block had given her as a souvenir of their encounter. Before she entered the house, she pulled out the strip of paper on which Block had written his cell phone number. She thought about ripping it up, telling Nikole, and contacting the police, but she dismissed the thought and tucked the number back into her pants pocket and headed into the house.

"Hey, girl! Where you been all day?" Nikole asked as she placed the dishes in the dishwater.

"You know, I had to get down with my brother today. You remember I told you yesterday about his birthday?" China said, pulling a carton of juice from the fridge and pouring some in a glass.

"Oh yeah. I totally forgot." Nikole had met Chase only one time, and that was years earlier, when he accompanied her to a gathering one of the girls had. She remembered how close they were.

"What's been going on around here all day?" China asked, gulping the juice down.

"I just got back in from dropping Curtis off at the airport. His agent got him on this national book tour that is starting out in New York in two days. He's touring from the east coast to the west coast and then coming down south. I really hate these long tours. I'm going to be without my boo for a whole month," Nikole said sadly while poking her bottom lip out.

"Why didn't you go with him?" China asked.

"Girl, I get so tired of the traveling and the hotel rooms. The last one I went with him on, I was stuck in the hotel room, bored out of my mind."

"Yeah, I feel you. Well, I guess we're going to have to find something to do to make the time fly by," China said, trying to block out the earlier situation with Block.

China hated betraying her friend, but she knew she had to carry out the plans. After taking to Nikole, she retreated to her room and called Block and told him of Curtis's coast-to-coast tour and how long he would be gone.

Later that night, Nikole invited China down to the TV room. They watched a series of Tyler Perry movies and sipped fancy wine.

"Girl, I love this part! Grit ball his ass!" Nikole screamed.

"Oh hell yeah!" China called out, laughing.

They laughed and had fun the whole night. After watching the third movie, they called it a night. Nikole headed to her bedroom while China retreated to the guest house, thinking about the dishonest and deceitful role she was being forced to play.

Chapter 20

B lock wasted no time putting his plans into action. He called China early Saturday morning and instructed her to get Nikole out of the house.

A couple hours later, Block sat outside the big iron gates in a darkly tinted Ford Taurus. He watched as the gates opened and a bright red BMW pulled out. After making sure they were well on their way, Block pulled up to the gate, entered the security code China had provided, and made his way up to the multimillion-dollar mansion.

After parking the car out front, Block made his way to the front door. He didn't hesitate to turn the knob and let himself in. He made a mental note to commend China for following his specific instructions, as he casually entered the hosue as if he lived there himself.

As he stepped in, he was more than impressed by the expensive furnishings and the state-of-the-art electronics that filled the house. Block walked through the house to make sure he was alone. After seeing that everything was clear, he made his way up to Nikole's bedroom.

Entering the bedroom, Block sniffed, taking in the scent of the White Diamonds perfume Nikole had been wearing for years. He searched his inside jacket pocket and pulled out a black envelope with gold trim on stationery he had hand picked just for this occasion. He walked over to the king-sized bed, but before he placed the envelope on the pillow, he pulled out the note and read it once more...

Hi, Nikole.

I've decided to let you live another day. I thought about hiding in your closet and waiting until you got comfortable before I jumped out like the big bad boogie man, but my plans have changed for you. I special delivered this letter right to your most intimate place—your bed. As you and I know, you betrayed me on every level, even burned down my house with the Aston I purchased just for you still in the garage. Being the nice guy that I am, I'm going to let you compensate me with money instead of your life. I want half a million delivered by tomorrow. Call me for the location. If you fail to meet my demands, I'm going to expose your previous life to your rich author husband and uppity high-class friends. They would really be surprised to find out that you were a sex toy for the rich. Nikole, it would be in your best interest to meet my demands, but if you decide differently, I will be forced to resort to my former plans, and you'll come up missing. Well, you have a good evening. I'll be waiting for your call. By the way... nice house.

Sincerely,
Block (678) 628-6674

Block smiled as he placed the letter back into the black and gold envelope and laid it on the overstuffed pillow. With part of his plan complete, he made his way back down to his car. As he pulled out of the iron gates, he admired the multimillion-dollar home through his rearview mirror.

Chapter 21

Nikole and China arrived back home hours later with a car full of designer clothes and shoes.

"Girl, I wish they would have had that new Gucci bag in stock. Now I'm going to have to stalk the store until they get it in," Nikole said playfully as she grabbed her bags and entered the house.

"You need to stop! You know that lil White girl is gonna call you as soon as they get it in. She's counting her commissions off that bag right now!" China jokingly fired back, at the same time wondering what Block had done in their absence.

"She better! Girl, I'm beat. I'm going to grab a

shower and lie back for a minute. If you need me for anything, just holla. I'll be in my room," Nikole told China as she slid off the three-inch heels and headed upstairs to her bedroom with her bags.

"Okay. I'm about to do the same," China responded as she headed to the guest house with her own shopping treasures.

Nikole placed her bags on the bedroom sofa and went to the bathroom to run some bath water. She stepped out of her pricey clothes as the oval-shaped tub filled with warm water. A couple minutes later, she was lying back in the tub with her eyes closed, as Monica sang from the wall-mounted, waterproof MP3 player. After bathing and relaxing for almost an hour, Nikole got out, dried herself off, and headed to her bed in the nude.

As Nikole reached the bed, she saw an envelope positioned on her pillow; it had not been there this morning when she left. Not knowing where it came from or how it got there, she picked it up and opened it cautiously and began to read...

Hi, Nikole.

I've decided to let you live another day...

Nikole's heart dropped as she continued to read the letter. Her thoughts ran wild as her head started to spin, and then the fear came. Nikole was shocked and scared. Snapping out of it, she ran to her closet, threw on some clothes, and bolted out of the door down to the guest house. "China! China!" Nikole screamed as she entered the guest house.

Just as Nikole was bursting in the door, China was hanging up the phone with Block, who gave her specific instructions for the second part of his plan.

"China, read this! We've got to get out of here!" Nikole screamed as she opened the envelope and pulled out the note for China to read.

After China read the letter with Block's demands, she insisted that Nikole pay Block off so he would leave her alone, which is what Block had instructed her to tell Nikole. "How in the hell did he find you?" China asked, playing the part. "He was in the house?" She felt so bad having to betray and lie to her friend.

"I... I don't know how... I just..." Nikole

stuttered, at a loss for words.

"Just give him what he wants so he will go away. I have some money saved up, so I can help. Let's pay him and get him out of our lives!" China stressed to Nikole, hoping she would agree.

"I'll take care of it if that is what it's going to take for him to leave me the fuck alone!" Nikole screamed, causing China to jump.

After talking to China, Nikole went back up to her bedroom and called the number on the bottom of the letter.

"Yeah?" Block answered, smiling from ear to ear, knowing it was Nikole and that his plan was underway.

"What do you want from me? Why don't you leave me the fuck alone?" Nikole screamed into the phone.

"Now, Nikole, is that a way to talk to someone who saved you from a crack whore mother who sold her little girl to get high? No, bitch, you listen and listen good. You get me that money by tomorrow night. I know your rich author husband don't know his lovely, beautiful wife used to be a fuck toy to whoever was willing to pay the price. Bitch, you owe me your life!" Block said heatedly.

"But you—" Nikole started.

"Shut the fuck up and listen! Bella will be at Lenox Mall in the food court tomorrow at three. Be there with the money. I know you are not stupid enough to involve the police when you know I service a majority of the force, all the way up to that damned horny-ass captain. Now, be a good little bitch and follow directions, and after this, I'll call it even and be out of your life," said Block.

"Block, how am I supposed to come up with that kind of—"

"Tomorrow at three!" Block yelled, cutting her off, and then he hung up the phone.

Nikole sat in her bedroom recliner and thought of a way to get Block the money. She and Curtis shared an account, so he would surely miss half a million dollars. Nikole knew she would have to meet Block's demands, or he would definitely expose her and ruin her life with Curtis. Nikole thought some more, and then it hit her. The safe! Nikole walked over to the expensive oil painting of Curtis and her.

She unsnapped the latch that held it securely over the digital wall safe. After entering the combination to the fireproof, air-tight safe, it popped open, revealing important documents and Curtis's $900,000 John Jay Pittman coin collection.

Nikole devised a plan to replace the real ones with some replicas until she could get the money saved up for another collection, or if she got lucky, she might even be able to buy them back, but for now, she just wanted to get Block out of her life for good. After going over her plans for the coins once again, she called China up to her room.

"You are a genius, girl!" China told Nikole after hearing the details of her plans to replace the coins.

The next morning, Nikole scouted around for replicas. After almost giving up, she found a dealer out in Sandy Springs that sold replica coins and had a match. Nikole rushed out to the shop, bought the replicas, and returned home. She unlocked the safe, pulled out the originals, and placed them in a bag. She then positioned the fake coins in the tray. After making sure everything was in order, she called Block.

"Yeah?" Block answered, knowing it was Nikole on the other end.

"I don't have the money, Block, but I have something that is worth a whole lot more than half a million," she said humbly.

Block sat up in his desk chair. "What is it?" he asked firmly.

"I have a coin collection worth almost a million. That's all I could come up with on such short notice," Nikole said faintly.

"A coin collection? I don't fuckin' collect coins! I want cash!" Block screamed into the phone.

"Block, right now I don't have that kind of cash. This coin collection is worth double what you asked me for. Block, please work with me. This is all I have!" Nikole cried.

Block thought for a minute and then put Nikole on hold while he pulled out his digital Rolodex and looked up a client from long ago that dealt in coins. After finding the client's contact info, he asked Nikole about the coins.

"It's a John Jay Pittman collection estimated at $900,000. That's all I know. Block, please work with me. This is all I have right—"

"I'll call you back!" Block spat, cutting Nikole off mid-sentence. He then dialed the little nerdy collector that always requested the biggest Black girls Block employed.

"Money in the bank, Mr. Block. That's a rare collection straight out of Egypt," the collector told Block.

"Can I get a flat million for it?" Block asked bluntly.

"Without a doubt. Matter of fact, I know a coin dealer out west that would happily give you a million for the collection, no questions asked."

"Hold that thought. I'll get back with you in a minute," Block said hastily as he ended the call and dialed Nikole's number.

"Hello?" Nikole answered.

"Bella will be waiting for you in the food court at three. Be there with the coins. Let me warn you... if you try anything funny, I promise you I won't be so lenient next go-'round," Block threatened.

"Nothing funny, Block. I just want to live my life. Please just leave me alone after I pay you!" Nikole pleaded.

"This will make us even. Have a nice life," Block said as he ended the call.

Block called the collector back and arranged a meeting for the next day, and then he called Bella. "Food court at three," he told her after giving her all the details about the payoff.

"I'll be there," Bella replied, more excited about seeing Nikole, who was like a daughter to her, than getting the payoff.

Chapter 22

As Bella sat in the food court waiting for Nikole, she thought about old times when Nikole first came to stay with her.

"Hey, little lady. What's your name?" Bella asked young Nikole, who was well developed for her age.

"Nikole," Nikole answered shyly.

"My name is Bella, and I'm going to teach you everything you need to know about surviving in this crazy world. First, let me show you your new room."

From the time Nikole moved, Bella was like a second mother to her. Out of all the girls Bella helped Block school, Nikole was the youngest and the one

Bella loved most like a daughter. At the young age of twenty-one, Bella found out that she could never bare children, so when young Nikole came along, she was the daughter Bella had always wanted. Bella taught Nikole every trick in the book and also schooled her on pleasing a man mentally and physically. Bella wanted Nikole to be everything she couldn't be. When China informed her and Block of Nikole's new life and pregnancy, she wanted to jump for joy, but at the same time, she wanted to silence China forever for giving up Nikole's location because she knew Block would surely go after Nikole. Bella couldn't wait to see Nikole and hoped Block would let her live her life peacefully after the payoff.

Bella sat in front of a Chinese food restaurant, thumbing through different apps on her Blackberry when Nikole approached her table.

"Hey, Bella," Nikole said dryly as she stood in front of the table holding the bag of coins.

"Nikole!" Bella cried out excitedly, happy to see her.

"Here's y'all money," Nikole spat as she laid the

bag on the table in front of Bella.

"Nikole, how have you been?" Bella asked in a concerned tone.

"Y'all have y'all money. Now please leave me alone," Nikole said angrily as she turned to walk off.

"Wait! Nikole!" Bella called out.

"Yeah?" Nikole said, turning back around.

"I need to talk to you. Come sit down," Bella insisted.

Nikole hesitantly sat in the chair facing Bella. Ever since the day Nikole was taken in by Block, she had seen Bella as a mother, and now she saw her in that same light. Tears welled up in Nikole's eyes as Bella reached over and grabbed her hand.

"Nikole, I'm sorry. As you and I both know, Block is a no-nonsense man and will go above and beyond until he's satisfied. Nikole, trust me, this is not my doing. Remember, one time, I used to be in your shoes. Baby, I only want the best for you and for you to be happy. I would never hurt you. I'm going to deliver this bag to Block, and you'll be able to live your life without any more distractions from this end. I just wanted to let you know that I love you like a daughter and miss you dearly. Please don't hate me for this, because, as you know, me and Block got history, and I can admit he literally saved my life. I'll always be grateful to him for that. My loyalty to him has no boundaries. I hate being stuck in between two people I love and care about deeply. Nikole, I'm sorry. Now go live your life and be the great mother I know you can be. Please keep in touch," Bella said, reaching into her purse and pulling out a business card to hand to Nikole.

"I will. I promise," Nikole said faintly as she wiped the tears from her eyes while she got up to walk off.

Bella grabbed the bag of coins and headed in the opposite direction on her way to meet with Block.

Chapter 23

Bella met Block at the Waffle House up the street from the mall. Bella spotted Block's dark tinted SUV as she pulled into the parking lot. She parked next to his truck, in the rear of the lot. Still upbeat from her rendezvous with Nikole, she grabbed the bag that contained the coins and got in the truck with Block.

"What do we have here?" Block inquired as he opened the bag and inspected the coins.

"These are worth a million?" Bella asked as she plucked a couple from the bag that Block held.

"They better be, or Nikole will be seeing me again real soon," Block said firmly as he held one of the coins up to inspect it closer.

"What's next?" Bella asked, watching Block inspect coin after coin.

"Turning these into cash," Block answered while he put the coins back in the bag and secured them under the seat.

"Sounds good to me. Now that you've settled the score with Nikole and China, we can get the ball rolling again with the service, right?" Bella said with enthusiasm.

"Yeah, but my plans don't end here," Block said, flashing a devious smile.

"What do you mean?" Bella asked curiously.

"I mean, if Nikole could come up with a million dollars' worth of coins in less than twenty-four hours, just think what else that little bitch could come up with. Her author husband is very well off, and I know a couple more million won't make him or break him. Besides, we could retire after that," Block smiled.

"Block, we are in the escort business, not the blackmail or extortion business. Let's just get the money off these coins and get back to work with the service."

"Bella, you and I know the escort business ain't what it used to be. Clients aren't paying top dollar for pussy no more. Then you got all these knock-off asshole escort services popping up everywhere, and they literally giving pussy away!" Block fired back.

"Well, we just going to have to step it up and start giving a lil pussy away too!" Bella fired back.

"Fuck that! One more lick like this, we can kick back on the platinum coast and count our money. Just look at it like this… we are already well off, but when we add a couple more million to the pot, ain't no looking back!" Block barked as he pulled out his phone and scrolled through the contact list looking for the collector's number.

"Block, we can turn the service around and make it a money-maker again like it used to be. First of all, we need to replace all these tired-ass, played-out hoes. Then we need to reach out for some new clientele. It won't be hard at all," Bella explained, hoping he would agree.

"We making Nikole come up with five more million, case closed," Block said in a firm, serious tone as he dialed the collector.

Bella sat in silence, trying to think of a way to convince Block otherwise as he talked to the collector. She had promised Nikole that she wouldn't have any further problems from Block after the money was paid, but now Block was preparing to go back for more. Bella waited until Block ended the call with the collector and then snapped, "I ain't with this shit!" She was frustrated and unable to think of any way to make Block change his mind.

"What?!" Block yelled as he ended the call with the collector.

"Like I said, I ain't with this shit!" Bella screamed as she opened the truck door and jumped out.

Block, becoming angry, opened his door and got out behind her. "Look here… we going to get this other five mill and retire, so deal with it!" Block spat heatedly as Bella opened her car door to get in.

"Block, I ain't with this blackmail shit!" Bella yelled as she got into her car.

"I'll call you with the plan tonight," Block snapped as he turned and walked back to his truck.

Block and the collector had agreed to meet later in the evening. After meeting with the collector, they went together to present the coins to a buyer. Block smiled from ear to ear as the buyer handed him a check for $980,000. Block paid the collector for his services, dropped him off at his car, and called Bella.

"Yeah, Block?" Bella answered in an irritated tone.

"Everything's good. I'm depositing $100,000 in your account in the morning," Block told her as he sat behind his office desk smoking a fat Cuban cigar.

"Block, I'm still against going back to Nikole for more money. We good with what we have. Just let Nikole be," Bella pleaded, hoping Block would give in.

"You going soft on me in your old age? The Bella I used to know would be totally down with getting this easy money, but you got a conscience. Look, just suck it up and get prepared. Now, listen, this is the plan…" he said firmly.

Block ran the plan down to Bella. She would play a major role. She started to flat out refuse, but she knew she couldn't refuse Block and be at peace. She was going to be included no matter what, so she prepared herself to go back to Nikole for more.

Chapter 24

The first masked man checked the rounds in his Glock 40 while the second masked man entered the code to the big iron gates outside of Nikole's home. It was two thirty in the morning, the best time to deliver a very urgent message from Block. As the gates creaked open, the masked man put the van in 'Drive' and eased through the gates with the van lights off. Inside the house, Nikole and China were knocked out after sipping wine and watching eighties reruns all night.

The two masked men, dressed all in black, slid out of the van and up to the front door. Block had given China specific instructions to leave the front door unlocked. The masked man turned the knob, and the door didn't open. After looking around and not finding any other way to get into the house without waking the occupants, they retreated back to the van and called Block.

"Yeah?" Block answered groggily.

"Hey, Mr. Block. We can't get in. The door is locked. We can break a window, but that's fo' sho' gonna wake everybody up. I thought you said the door was gonna be open?" the gunman whispered softly.

"The door wasn't unlocked?" Block asked, perturbed.

"Naw. We sitting out front right now."

"Hold up for a minute. I'll call you right back." Block hung up and quickly dialed China's cell phone number.

China answered on the third ring. "Hello?" she said, half-asleep.

"Bitch, you didn't follow my instructions!"

"Hold up! Block, what's wrong?" China asked in a frightened tone.

"Why the fuck ain't the front door open?" Block

screamed into the receiver.

"Damn! I totally forgot, Block. I'm sorry. I'm getting up right now. Sorry, Block!" China said sincerely as she hung up and hurried through the house to unlock the front door. As she unlatched the security chain, she heard some footsteps coming up behind her. Quickly turning, she looked right Nikole's face.

"What's up, China? What you doing?" Nikole asked, confused.

China was lost for words. "Oh, I needed to—"

Before China could get the words out of her mouth, the front door slammed open, knocking her down. Nicole screamed at the top of her lungs when the two masked men rushed through the door with guns drawn. Nikole got to the kitchen before she was grabbed from behind and slammed to the floor. The other man snatched China up from behind the door and dragged her into the kitchen, where the other man had Nicole laying face down with his pistol to the back of her head.

"So we meet again?" the masked man said to China with his eyes fixated on her double Ds that showed through her sheer nightgown.

"I don't know what you're talking about!" China responded, hoping Block had told the men about her working with him undercover.

"She the girl with the brother. Yeah, I remember her," the other masked man said, still pointing the gun in the back of Nikole's head.

Nikole was shocked to know China actually knew the men, but she wondered what they wanted with her.

"Look here, Nikole. You need to meet Block's demand by the weekend. Don't try to run and hide, because we will hunt you down and kill you if you do," said the man with the gun to her head.

"Please! I already paid Block. I swear I paid him!" Nikole cried, shocked they were after her.

"Oh, I forgot to tell you them coins were fake, and now Block wants five million," said the other gunman that stood over China with his pistol pointed at her.

"Please don't hurt us! I will get his damn money," Nikole cried.

"I don't want to have to make a second trip out

here. Next time, it won't be your friend who is losing her life… it will be you," the man said, pushing the gun harder into the back of her head.

"What are you talking about?" Nikole asked.

"This."

As soon as the man responded, the other masked man standing over China fired two shots point blank, right into her face.

"Noooo! Noooo!" Nikole screamed as China's blood splattered over toward her, soaking her clothes.

"By the weekend!" the two men said again as they rushed out of the front door, back to the van. A few minutes later, they were on 285, heading back to the west side of Atlanta.

Nikole shook uncontrollably as she dialed 911. When the police arrived, she told them two masked men had burst into the house and robbed them and shot China when she tried to fight back. Nikole never mentioned Block's name, scared of what he might do to her if she did.

The next day, China's murder was all over the news, and best-selling author Curtis Conway had also caught wind of it. Curtis cancelled his book tour and flew home immediately. On the way back from picking Curtis up from the airport, Nikole sobbed all the way home, thinking about China and the five million she had to come up with.

Chapter 25

"Block, you fuckin' insane!" Bella screamed as they sat in Block's office reading about the robbery/murder at the famous author's mansion.

"Everything is cool. Sometimes you have to let people know you are serious," Block said in a menacing tone.

"Serious? Serious! You're going absolutely too far with this shit! What's gotten into you, Block?" Bella screamed as she paced the floor.

Block sat in silence as Bella ranted and raved about the murder. He waited for her to calm down a bit before he spoke. "There's no doubt Nikole will come up with the five million. Just think of it like this… China guaranteed that we're gonna have money in the bank."

"You had her killed! That was not necessary at all! We could have gotten Nikole to pay without killing China. Do you know how much trouble we will be in if Nikole goes to the police?" Bella asked, sitting down on the plush black sofa.

"She won't talk," Block said assuredly, rearing back in his oversized leather office chair.

"You better hope not!" Bella screamed.

Bella and Block sat in his office for hours, booking dates for the girls and going over accounts. Block had an important meeting with a potential rich client, so he left Bella in his office to continue booking dates.

An hour later, Bella had booked $40,000 worth of dates and updated all the behind accounts. Making sure she had taken care of everything, she grabbed her purse, cut off the office lights, and headed home.

As she headed down Peachtree Street en route to her place, Bella thought about poor Nikole. After entertaining thoughts of her surrogate daughter, she decided to give her a call.

"Hello?" Nikole answered faintly.

"Hey, Nikole. This is Bella. I need to—"

"How could you let this happen, Bella? You promised me everything would be okay!" Nikole cried as she stood in her living room looking out the back window at the manmade pool with a beautiful waterfall.

"Nikole, I swear I had no idea of Block's plans. Nikole… just… please be careful."

"Bella, I don't have five million to pay Block. How am I going to come up with that kind of money in two days? Bella, I'm scared! Please help me," Nikole sobbed.

Bella didn't know what to do. She knew Block was serious about the five million, and she knew he would go to extremes to get it. She hated to tell Nikole there was nothing she could do. "Nikole," she said, "I will try to speak with Block." It was all she could say, as she wiped a tear from her eye.

"Bella, I paid him! Then these men say the coins were fake! I know they were real. They killed China, Bella!" Nikole cried.

"Yeah, Nikole. I hate that it has come to this,"

Bella said as she turned onto her street.

"He'll always want more! I'm not paying. He can fucking kill me or tell everybody about my past. I don't fucking care! He will always want more, Bella!" Nikole screamed.

"Nikole, I don't think that's—"

Click! Nikole hung up before Bella could finish.

Bella tried dialing her number back, but it went straight to voicemail. She decided right then to get away from it all. She didn't want to be around when Nikole ended up hurt—maybe even dead—for not paying Block. As soon as she stepped into her place, she started packing everything she needed for her getaway to the Virgin Islands. She had enough money stashed away to stay there until everything blew over. She would tell no one where she was going. She would simply disappear.

Chapter 26

"You okay?" Curtis asked, rushing into the living room after hearing Nikole scream.

"I'm okay," Nikole told Curtis as he took her into his arms.

"They are going to find out who did this. I got some security people coming over tomorrow to install the best system money can buy. You won't have to worry about that ever again, baby," Curtis assured Nikole as he held her tight.

"Thanks," Nikole whispered, knowing she would need more than a security system to keep herself alive.

"How about getting out of the house for a while?

Let's go on a vacation," Curtis insisted.

"Nah. I'm not really up to it, baby. I just need to lie down," Nikole said, pulling away from Curtis and walking out of the room, heading to her bedroom.

Curtis trailed behind her but made a detour to his downstairs office. Pulling the door up behind him, he rushed over to his stash spot under his office couch and pulled out his glass pipe and lighter. Curtis positioned the small white rock on the tip of the pipe and put the flame to it.

Just as he was taking another hit, Nikole walked through the door to let him know his agent was on the phone. "What in the hell are you doing?" Nikole asked in disbelief as Curtis stood there with the glass pipe and the lighter in his hands. Nikole's heart dropped. All she could see was her mother at the old wooden table in the rooming house, smoking on the glass pipe with different men that would climb in bed with her at her mother's direction.

"Oh... okay... I'm... I'm on—"

Before Cutis could get his words out, Nikole was on him, hitting him with everything she had. Curtis tried his best to restrain her, but he couldn't. She landed blow after blow. She punched, kicked, and scratched him until a sharp pain in her stomach sent her crashing to the floor.

Curtis regained his composure and bent down to help her.

"Leave me alone! Don't touch me!" Nikole screamed as she held her stomach.

"Come on, Nikole! I'm sorry! Let me help you!"

"Get away from—"

Nikole had passed out. When she woke up, she was in South Fulton Hospital, being treated for a miscarriage. Nikole couldn't hold back the tears when the doctor informed her that she had lost her baby. Nikole hated her life right now. Her rich, famous husband was on crack, she lost her baby, and her life was on the line for five million dollars that she didn't have. She let the tears flow freely from her eyes as she drifted back off to sleep.

The next morning, when she woke up, Curtis was standing by her bed, rubbing her head.

"Please leave, Curtis," Nikole spat groggily.

"Nikki, I'm so sorry. I really need help," Curtis said, quivering as he spoke.

"I can't believe you! I always thought you were a stronger man than that!" Nikole snapped.

"I'm going to get help, I swear."

"I can't do this, Curtis," Nikole said, lying back on the hard hospital pillow and closing her eyes.

"I'm checking into rehab. It's just... just so hard," Curtis stammered.

Later that night, Nikole was released from the hospital. She and Curtis rode home in silence while Anita Baker sang "Sweet Love" from the expensive Mercedes sound system.

When they reached home, Nikole went straight to her bedroom without saying a word as Curtis detoured to the game room to watch TV and think. When Nikole reached her room, she snatched her clutch bag off the black leather recliner and dumped all of its contents on the bed. She fished through her belongings until she found the letter with Block's phone number written on the bottom. She grabbed her cell phone off the nightstand and dialed.

"Yeah?" Block answered, smiling to himself, reasoning that he was about to become five million dollars richer.

"Hey, Block. I have your money—all cash and big bills like you instructed. Where do I meet you?" Nikole asked humbly.

"I'll have Bella contact you in a minute."

"No! I'm not meeting with anyone but you. I don't want any excuses this time," Nikole insisted.

"Oh okay. No problem. Just come to the house then," Block told her.

"I'll be there tomorrow at one, but you have to give me your word you will leave me alone after this," Nikole ordered.

"You have my word. I will let you be," Block said sincerely as he pulled up in his driveway.

"I'll be there," Nikole said and hung up the phone.

Chapter 27

Lying on the bed that night with Curtis fast asleep next to her, Nikole went over her plans in her head over 100 times before falling asleep.

The next morning when she awoke, Curtis was sitting at his desk writing. "Good morning," he called out after hearing her stir in her bed.

"Good morning," Nikole reluctantly replied as she got up out of the bed and went into the kitchen.

Ten minutes later, she came out of the bathroom with her hair tied back in a ponytail, looking distraught.

"Where are you going?" Curtis asked as he continued to type on his computer.

"Out for a minute," Nikole fired back as she put on her oversized Nike jogging suit and tennis shoes.

Curtis didn't respond, knowing he would only get more attitude from Nikole.

She pulled her shoelaces tight and exited the room. She grabbed her gym bag out of the closet in the game room and headed to the garage. There, she opened the gym bag and filled it with old newspapers and a few of Curtis's paperback books. After stuffing the bag full, she reached into Curtis's car window and opened his glove box and grabbed the .38 revolver that she knew he kept there for protection. After making sure she had everything, she climbed into her BMW, went over her plans once again, and then pulled out of the garage to head for Block's house.

Twenty minutes later, she was pulling up into his driveway. Placing the gun in her sweat suit jacket pocket, she grabbed the duffle bag full of old newspapers and books and headed up to Block's front door.

NikoleknewshewasundersurveillancebyBlock's twenty-four-hour security guard who lived in his basement and watched the security monitors all day.

Before she could knock, the front door was pulled open by Block, who stood there looking down at Nikole in an eggshell white linen suit and loafers. "Come on in, Nikole. It's good to see you," Block said, flashing a phony smile.

Nikole didn't say anything. She simply stepped past him into the house with the gym bag tight in her grip.

"Come down to my office so we can handle this and be out of each other's hair," Block said as he led the way to his office.

As they entered the office, Nikole walked over to stand in front of the office window while Block took a seat behind his desk. "Why did you have China killed?" she whispered, dropping the gym bag next to her.

"She was not trustworthy. How did you think we found you in the first place?" Block told Nikole as he pulled out a cigar from his desk drawer and lit it.

"This is where it all ends, Block," Nikole said softly.

"Yeah, it is. You have my word. Now, bring the bag over here so we can make sure all the money is in there first," Block instructed as he exhaled the thick cigar smoke.

"No, Block. *This* is where it all ends!" Nikole screamed as she pulled the .38 from her jacket and pointed at her unsuspecting former boss.

"Whoa! Hold up now, Nikole!" Block called out, dropping his cigar as he stood up behind his desk.

"Block, I refuse to live as your slave! I know when you blow the five million, you'll be back for more!" Nikole screamed as tears ran down her face.

"Look, Nikole, just calm down and put the gun away," Block said softly with his hands in the air.

Pop!

Gun smoke filled the air, and the room went dark.

Chapter 28

Nikole lay on the ground bleeding, holding her leg in pain.

"You okay, boss?" Block's private security guard asked with his smoking gun still pointed at Nikole.

"Yeah, I'm fine, but I need you to do me a favor. Get in touch with Dr. Kelsey and tell him I need to see him immediately. Tell him it's a gunshot wound," Block said while walking over to Nikole, who was breathing hard, holding her leg in pain.

"So this is how you want it, Nikole? We could have done this a better way, but no… you chose this road!" Block barked as he walked over and picked up Nikole's gun and tucked it into his waist.

"Fuc… Ahhh!" Nikole screamed out in pain.

"Just remember, you wanted it this way," Block told her as he stepped over her and grabbed the gym bag. He carried the bag to his desk, set it down, and unzipped it. "Bitch!" he screamed as he dumped the newspapers and Curtis's books on his desk. He rushed over to Nikole, who was still squirming around on the floor, crying and holding her leg in pain. "Bitch, you don't like living! Where the fuck is my money?" Block screamed as he pulled her gun from his waist and pointed it at her.

"Just kill me! I don't care! I… ahh! Do it!" Nikole screamed, holding her leg.

"Nah, I got a better idea. We going to see how much your rich author husband is willing to pay to get his lovely wife back," Block smirked.

"Leave him out… ahh… of this! I hate your no-good, murd… ahh!"

Block put the gun back in his waist and walked back over to his desk, where he picked up the phone and dialed Bella's number.

The voicemail picked up on the third ring. "Hi. This is Bella. Sorry I…"

"Bella, come to the house as soon as possible. Our lil friend Nikole paid us a visit, but now she is going to be our guest for a while until her husband comes to get her. As soon as you get this, head this way," Block said before he sent it as an urgent message.

On the other side of town, headed to the airport, Bella ignored Block's call. After he hung up, she saw that he had left a voicemail. Curious, she listened and cringed when he said he had Nikole at the house. Bella knew Nikole wouldn't leave there alive, and she didn't know what to do.

"Boss, the doc is on the way. You need me for anything else?" the security guard asked.

"No. I'm good. Just show the doc in when he arrives. I'll be out back in the guest house."

Block picked Nikole up like a ragdoll and carried her out back to the guest house against her will.

The doc arrived a few minutes later and was escorted back by the security guard. "What we got here?" he asked, putting on his glasses to get a closer look at Nikole's wound. After seeing what needed to be done, the doc pulled latex gloves from his bag and went to work on Nikole. Fifteen minutes later, Nikole was bandaged up and woozy from pain medication.

"Thanks, doc. I'll be in touch," Block said as he handed the doctor a wad of bills.

A few minutes later, the security guard walked through the door to escort him out.

"Anytime," the doc replied as he followed the security guard out.

After seeing the doctor out, the security guard returned. "I'll be watching the monitors. Just holla if you need me, boss."

"A'ight," Block responded.

After the security guard left the room, Block walked over to Nikole, who was lying on the couch, heavily sedated. "Well, Nikole, we can do this the hard way or the easy way."

"Fuck you!" she slurred.

Slap! Block hit her and then smashed her head into the arm of the couch. "Listen here, you disloyal tramp, one way or the other, I'm going to get what's due me," Block spat as he held her head tightly against the sofa.

Nikole's pain medication slightly impacted

Block's assault, but she knew if she didn't cooperate, more was to come. "Wa... okay... jus..." she slurred as Block used both hands to press her face deeper and deeper into the upholstery.

The pain medication had taken its toll, and Nikole couldn't free herself from Block's grip. On top of that, she felt dizzy. A few seconds later, all she could see was darkness; she was out cold.

After Nikole blacked out, Block got some duct tape from the house and bound her hands behind her back. Satisfied she couldn't get out of the tape, he picked up the guest house phone and dialed his security guard.

"Yeah, boss?"

"Keep an eye on her. Alert me when she wakes up," Block instructed.

"Okay. Got ya, boss."

Leaving the guest house, Block went into his office and called his messengers.

Chapter 29

Later that night, Curtis sat in the game room watching LeBron battle Kobe. Noticing it was getting late, he picked up the phone and dialed Nikole's cell phone. When he didn't get an answer, he started to get worried. He knew she was still mad at him about his drug problem, but it was not like her to ignore her phone. Hearing a noise, Curtis peeked out the window and saw Nikole's red BMW pulling through the big iron gates. Relieved that she was home, he focused his attention back on the game.

The driver used the automatic garage door opener to open the garage while the passenger loaded his nine-millimeter and pulled down his ski mask. The driver pressed the button to close the garage and then pulled his own ski mask over his head. In a split second, they were in the house going from room to room, looking for Curtis.

After searching the second floor with no luck, they headed downstairs. Just as they hit the bottom step, they heard a TV and somebody rooting for someone to shoot the ball. The two men slowly rounded the corner and saw Curtis sitting with his back to them. He was sipping on a beer with his feet up on the coffee table, watching a basketball game. They rushed him from behind and pinned him to the floor.

"Wha! Hey! Hey!!" Curtis screamed as the masked intruders held him down, waving their guns in his face.

"Look here, man! Just cooperate, and you won't be hurt," the first masked man said firmly.

"Okay. What… what do you want?" Curtis asked shakily.

"We are here to deliver a very important message," the second masked man said.

Instantly, Curtis remembered Nikole's BMW.

"Where's my wife?" he yelled.

"Shut up and listen! Your wife is being held until you meet our demands. As soon as you meet our demands, she will be free to go," the first gunman explained as he pressed his weapon into the side of Curtis's face.

"Wait! Okay!" Just tell me what I need to do," Curtis asked humbly as sweat rolled off his forehead.

"We want eight million in cash, non-negotiable," the first masked man announced.

"Eight million? Where am I gonna get—"

Before Curtis could finish, the first masked man struck him in the head with the butt of his nine-millimeter, splitting the side of his face open.

"Eight million if you want to see your wife again. And oh, I forgot to inform you that includes saving your own life as well," the second masked man stressed.

The two men had been instructed by Block to deliver the five-million-dollar message, but on the way over to the job, they decided to add three million to line their own pockets. As far as they were concerned, Block's pay was way too low for the work they were putting in.

"Y'all look… I don't have eight million in cash, but I got valuables that's worth the eight million. Please just accept them. I have a lil cash, but the rest got to be in valuables," Curtis begged.

The two masked men looked at each other like they could read each other's minds, and they decided to see what Curtis had to offer.

"Okay. Let's see what you got," the first masked man said as he let Curtis up.

Curtis slowly got up and pressed his shirt to the side of his bleeding face. He led the men up to his bedroom, where his wall safe was. Shaking, he unlatched the picture that hid the safe and entered the code. As soon as the safe popped open, the men pushed Curtis to the side.

"What do we have here?" the second masked man asked as he pulled the tray of coins from the shelf.

"How much these worth?" the other masked man asked.

"It's listed on the tray, but since then, their value has increased considerably," Curtis lied, knowing the value of the coins was still the same."

"One point one million!" the man called out, looking at the tag on the tray.

"Okay. Seven million to go," the first masked man said.

After watching them bag up the coins, Curtis led them to his other safe, which was stored in his office. The safe contained cash and expensive jewelry. When he reached the office, he walked over to his computer desk and moved it over to reveal a floor safe. After he entered the combination code, he moved to the side and watched as the two men ripped out the contents.

"There's $600,000 in cash, two diamond Rolex watches, a diamond bracelet, and a diamond ring," the first masked man called out as he inventoried the contents of the safe.

"What do you think this stuff's worth?" the second masked man asked.

"Man, I don't fucking know!" the first man barked.

"What's this shit worth? And if you lie, I promise you and your wife will be killed," the first man screamed.

"The jewelry is easily worth over three million, I swear," Curtis assured the man.

"I can go for that. So, that's three million plus the $600,000 in cash, plus the million worth of coins, so now we looking for three million more, mister!" the second man called out.

"The only thing I have left is the Picasso hanging in the living room. It's worth two and a half million, easy," Curtis said faintly.

"Okay. Lead the way," the man told Curtis, motioning at him with his gun.

When they reached the living room, Curtis pulled a chair over and stood on it and reluctantly removed his prized possession and passed it down to the men.

"We appreciate your cooperation. Like I told you when you arrived, you meet our demands, and we will release your wife. I will make the call now," the second masked man said as he pulled his cell phone from his pocket and dialed Block's number.

"Yeah?"

"Everything cool. Money in the bank."

"Alright. Just meet me in an hour at Ed's Barbershop down on Peachtree Street," Block said, proudly counting the five million in his head.

"We'll be there," the man said and hung up.

Before leaving, they tied Curtis up in a kitchen chair. They removed their masks as they loaded the valuables into Nikole's BMW and headed out to meet Block.

"Man, we got eight million dollars' worth of shit here," the second man said, looking back in the back seat.

"Yeah, this cheap-ass nigga giving us $100,000 a piece when we putting in all this work," the driver said.

"I'm tired of working for peanuts," the second man said.

"Matter of fact, fuck this nigga!" the driver screamed as he turned the car around and headed back toward the west side, their side of town.

Chapter 30

After getting the call from the messengers, Block went out to the guest house and untied Nikole. "I guess your rich husband loves his wife. You're free to go," Block said, opening the side door so Nikole could leave.

Nikole could barely walk, but she made it up to the corner store and used the pay phone to call a cab.

Two hours had passed, and Block hadn't heard from the messengers. He had arrived at the barbershop way ahead of time. He had made several calls to both of their cell phones, but he only got their voicemails. Block stood out in front of the barbershop, impatiently waiting for his employees to show up. He cursed under his breath, knowing something wasn't right. He cursed as he got into his truck. He pulled out his cell and dialed Bella's number and got no answer from her either.

Block didn't know what was going on. He started the truck and headed out to Bella's place. Arriving a few minutes later, he got out and rushed up to the front door. After knocking and not getting an answer, he went around back and looked in. The scene was familiar: open drawers, empty closets and doors, Bella was gone.

"Fuck!" Block spat as he returned to his truck. He didn't know what was going on, and everything was falling apart. He tried calling his messengers again, and there was still no answer. Frustrated and confused, he rushed home to think.

Block sat behind the desk and thought of his next move. He was sure the messengers had run off with his money. He vowed to recover his money at all costs. With his mind made up, Block changed into his all-black Dickies suit and grabbed his Desert Eagle from his desk drawer. He tried calling his messengers one last time before heading to the west side to find them.

Block figured if he caught them soon enough, he would be able to recover most of the money. On his way to the west side, he made a couple calls to his connects, telling them to be on the lookout for Big D and Jesse, who were well known in the area. He also told his connects to be on the lookout for a new red BMW that would surely stand out in their 'hood.

Thirty minutes later, Block was exiting the freeway on MLK, headed down to the messengers' 'hood. Before Block reached the neighborhood, he got a call back from Shontay, an old employee and a good friend. She told him she was sure the BMW parked next door to her apartment was the one he was looking for. "Who stay next door?" Block asked, turning his stereo system down.

"Keisha, a stripper from up north that's working at Magic now," Shontay told him as she peeked out the window.

"Appreciate it. I'll holla later."

"Make sure you get back at me, Block," Shontay told him. She was still in love with the man that took her virginity.

A few minutes later, Block was pulling up next to the BMW. He got out of the truck and walked over to the red car. There was no sign of the men or the money. He walked up to the apartment door and knocked hard, summoning Keisha to the door with an attitude.

"Yeah? What?" she yelled as she snatched the door open.

"Back up!" Block snapped with the Desert Eagle pointed at her. He backed her up into the apartment and closed the door behind him. "Where are the men that's driving that car?" Block asked Keisha, who stood in the middle of her floor wearing nothing but a thin tank top and a pair of boy shorts that exposed her thick thighs.

"Man, I don't know what's going on. What are you—"

"Nigga, put the gun down!" Big D screamed from behind Block.

"Yeah, nigga, drop it!" Jesse barked as he stepped out of the closet where he had been hiding.

"So this is how y'all niggas roll after all I've done

for y'all? Look, man, let's just split that money up and forget all of this ever happened," Block said humbly as he placed the Desert Eagle back in his waist.

"Folks, put the gun down!" Jesse shouted.

"Hold up, bro… okay? Just chill!" Block uttered as he pulled the gun from his waist again. He knew he would not get out of the apartment alive unless he did something quick. "A'ight, man, y'all can have the money," Block said, lying the gun on the floor and cautiously turning to leave.

"Nah, bro," Jesse spat as he ordered Block to get down on the floor.

"Hey, y'all, I'm out, and don't be killing nobody in my apartment," Keisha said, stepping around Block headed to the door.

As soon as she got within arm's reach, Block grabbed her and in a swift motion swiped his gun up from the floor in front of him. "Look, niggas, this bitch die if y'all don't back the fuck down!"

"Nigga, fuck you and that bitch!" Jesse snapped as he squeezed the trigger, hitting Keisha and Block.

Jesse and Big D knew when they took the money

that Block would have to die, and they had already made plans to take him out. After watching Block and Keisha hit the floor, the two men bolted out the door and disappeared between the rundown apartments.

Hearing the gunshots and then seeing the men bolt from the apartment, Shontay called 911. Five minutes later, Keisha was pronounced dead on the scene, and Block was rushed to Grady Memorial, barely breathing.

Chapter 31

Thirty minutes later, Nikole hobbled up the doorstep and entered her house. She frantically called out Curtis's name. She prayed as she went from room to room that he was okay. After searching the rooms, she finally looked in the kitchen, where she found him tied up she ran over and untied him. "Baby!" she screamed as she scratched and pulled at the ropes and duct tape.

"Ah… Nikki…" he panted as she removed the sticky gray tape from his mouth.

Nikole cried as she cut the ropes that held him securely to the kitchen chair.

After he was freed, he took her into his arms and

held her tightly. "Damn, baby. I'm so glad you're okay. Thank you, Lord," Curtis said softly as he held Nikole, who couldn't stop crying. "We need to call the police," Curtis declared, springing up and walking over to the phone.

"No! Just let it be please!" Nikole pleaded, following closely behind him.

Stopping in his tracks, he turned and at Nikole. "Nikole, I need to know what is going on right now," he demanded as they stood face to face in the hallway.

Seeing the seriousness in his eyes, Nikole led him into the living room, where she told him everything. She started at her mother's drug habit and the rape by the different men at such a young age and continued on to working for Block's escort service.

Curtis was shocked at Nikole's revelations, but at the same time, he felt bad for her. He realized why she acted out like she did when she found him doing drugs. He promised her right then and there that he would get help for his drug habit, and he meant it. "It's not your fault," Curtis said softly as he cradled a crying Nikole.

Later that evening laying in bed, they were contacted by the Atlanta police department because their car was now linked to a murder scene. Curtis gave the detective a story about the car being borrowed by a friend. "Murder?" Curtis asked.

Nikole sat up in bed when she heard it.

"I hope my friend is okay," Curtis said, playing along.

"Well, we're sorry to say Keisha Walker is dead, multiple gunshot wounds to her upper torso," the detective explained.

"Damn!" Curtis said, still playing along.

"The guy—I think his name is Wilburn Gilbert—was rushed to Grady Hospital, in ICU."

"Wilburn Gilbert?" Curtis repeated, causing Nikole to grab his hand.

"Sir, after the investigation, you can recover your car from our impound yard. We'll contact you as soon as we process it and deem it is not needed for further investigation."

"Thanks. Just keep me informed," Curtis uttered as he hung up the phone.

"Did you say 'Wilburn Gilbert'?" Nikole asked,

sitting straight up in bed.

"Yeah. Probably one of the dudes that came in here," Curtis spat, pulling Nikole down on his chest.

"That's Block, the one I told you about! What happened?" Nikole asked, sitting back up.

Curtis relayed the message that the detective had given him, and she smiled to herself at the thought of Block stuck in intensive care. She said a silent prayer to herself, hoping he wouldn't pull through.

They lay in bed silently until they both fell fast asleep. The next morning when Curtis awoke, Nikole was gone.

"Hi. I'm here to see Wilburn Gilbert," the woman told the heavyset receptionist.

"Relation?" the receptionist asked.

"Sister," the woman dressed in all black and dark shades replied."

"Around the corner to the right."

"Thanks."

Reaching Block's room, the woman peeked in. When she saw he was alone, she entered and closed the door behind her. She walked over next to his bed, where he was hooked up to an IV and a breathing machine. She tapped him on the arm, causing his eyes to flutter open.

Block was shocked when he saw who was standing at his bedside. He tried to speak, but the words wouldn't come out. He could only lie there and gaze up at the woman helplessly.

The woman took out her handkerchief and dabbed the tears from her eyes. Regaining her composure, she leaned down and whispered in Block's ear, "I love you," as she reached over and disconnected the breathing machine that kept Block alive.

The woman hastily left the room and headed for the parking lot. After getting in her car, she speedily headed for the airport and thought about the peace that waited for her on the Ivory Coast. The thought of it all made Bella smile.

After hearing about Block's death Nikole said a silent prayer. She smiled as her and Bella ended their call, it was all over.

The End

PRESENTS

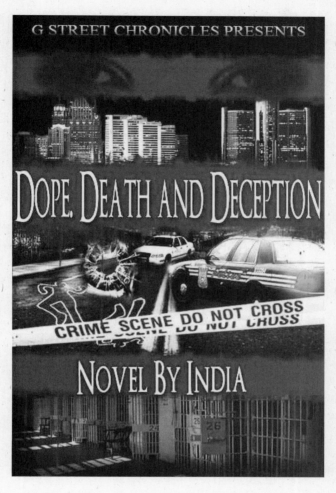

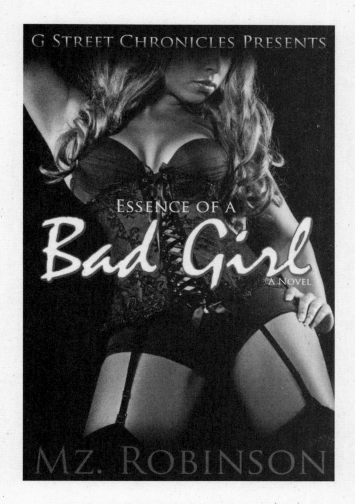

Visit www.gstreetchronicles.com
to view all of our titles.

Join us on Facebook
G Street Chronicles Fan Page

G STREET CHRONICLES PRESENTS

Drama

A Novel

George Sherman Hudson

Visit www.gstreetchronicles.com
to view all of our titles.

Join us on Facebook
G Street Chronicles Fan Page

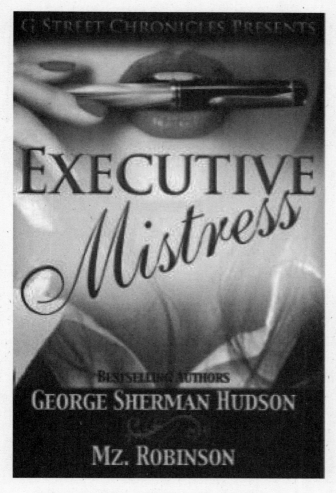

Visit www.gstreetchronicles.com
to view all of our titles.

Join us on Facebook
G Street Chronicles Fan Page

G Street Chronicles Presents

FAMILY Ties

A Novel

GEORGE SHERMAN HUDSON

Visit www.gstreetchronicles.com
to view all of our titles.

Join us on Facebook
G Street Chronicles Fan Page

Visit www.gstreetchronicles.com
to view all of our titles.

Join us on Facebook
G Street Chronicles Fan Page

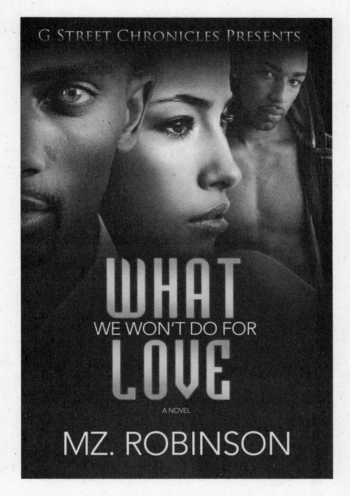

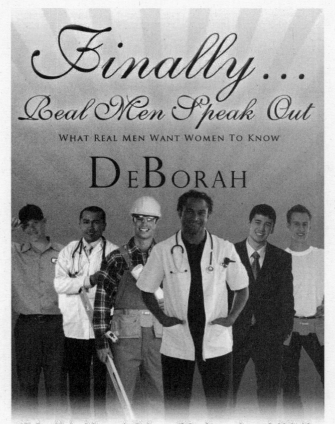